OPTURIUS
BENEATH A CRIMSON SKY

THE RED SKY TRILOGY

DAVE HAYES

dhayesMEDIA

Copyright © 2025 by Dave Hayes

All rights reserved.

This book is protected by the copyright laws of the United States of America. No part of this book may be reproduced in any form or by any electronic or mechanical means, including information storage and retrieval systems, without prior written permission from the author, except for the use of brief quotations in a book review.

Permission requests may be emailed to: davidjhayes@protonmail.com

ISBN: 978-1-966987-07-9 (DHayes Media)

Printed in the U.S.A.

For Danny and Diego

ACKNOWLEDGMENTS

I must thank my editor on this project, Lydia Posusta, for her months of hard and focused work on my draft manuscript. I appreciate the questions she asked and problems she highlighted, which forced me to create a better story. Her expertise on finessing the poem was instrumental as well as her suggestions to further develop the emotional story of the characters.

ONE

THE SKY LOOKED like a nuclear bomb had exploded, showering the terrain below in a haze of crimson. Adam Walker trekked along a narrow ridge heading east. The earth beneath his boots wasn't any soil he recognized. It crunched slightly, like dry scales, and shimmered with a metallic sheen. Strange plants lined the slope—thick-stemmed, and trembling in the warm breeze.

The wind whispered across the unfamiliar terrain, carrying the scent of ozone and pulverized stone. Far below, something chirred—a rhythm like clockwork—perhaps a strange insect hidden in the underbrush.

Adam crested the ridge and halted. Before him, the land fell away into a broad valley, cut through with a wide river that curled like a ribbon of blood. He heard a voice whisper.

He turned to his left and beheld a towering mountain range. The peaks were unknown to him, rising like jagged teeth against the horizon. The sky was illuminated by a massive, ruby sun. A planet easily three times the size of the moon hung 15 degrees above the mountains in the northern sky.

Adam gazed at the mountains. And then he woke.

He sat up in bed, sweat drenching his back, the sheets twisted at his knees. He swung his legs over the edge of the bed and rubbed his eyes. Light trickled in through the slits in the blinds. He yawned, stretched, and then stood, weaving between piles of clothes, and passing dirty paper plates on his way to the bathroom.

Adam had left the TV on with the volume down low. Sinatra was singing "Fly Me to the Moon." His mother sang big band music in a trio after graduating from high school before marrying Adam's father. He grew up listening to her favorite vocalists.

He splashed warm water on his face and quickly shaved. The images from the dream haunted him. He dried his face with a ratty hand-me-down towel he'd gotten from his mother.

Strangest mountains I've ever seen, he thought. *And what's with the red sky?*

And then, there was the river, which made him feel vulnerable. He headed for the kitchen. "Coffee first, alien mountain ranges later."

He walked into a tiny kitchen, poured water into the coffee maker, and ground a handful of fresh Sumatra beans, which he had chosen for their full-bodied, earthy flavor, with notes of chocolate, cedar, and vanilla. I may live in a dump, he told his girlfriend, but I don't have to drink crappy coffee. He emptied the grounds into the filter and pressed the "brew" button—and then it happened.

There was no sound. No warning of any kind. The room around him dissolved. Suddenly, he was in an unfamiliar house, standing over the blood-covered body of a dead woman.

Then, his vision shifted. A door was open before him, and he entered.

He stood in a dim hallway. The floor was covered with peeling linoleum. The walls were lined with warped wood paneling. Somewhere nearby, a dog barked.

Adam's vision shifted again, pulled toward a doorway at the end of the hall. He entered. The room beyond was silent. Mildew hung in the air. A man stood before him. He was thin and pale, in his late forties. His hands trembled slightly as he paced. A snake tattoo was visible on the left side of his neck. He muttered something unintelligible to himself.

The vision narrowed and pulled toward the window.

Now, Adam was outside, looking up at a red tin roof. It was old, rusted, and pocked with hailstone scars. The house was isolated, surrounded by tall, dry grass and the distant line of a quarry wall.

The vision slowly faded.

Adam was back in his kitchen. He rubbed his eyes once, then reached for the notebook on the counter and wrote:

> Dead woman. Snake tattoo on the left side of the neck. Red tin roof. Dog barking. Out past the quarry.

He quickly sketched the tattoo and the house, then set the pencil down.

The coffee maker beeped, ripping him from his thoughts. He sighed. "Another unsolved murder?" He slid the notepad aside and poured his coffee.

TWO

THE FERRY HAD DOCKED in Anacortes hours ago, but the rhythm of the sea still lingered in Adam's mind. He drove south toward Olympia with the windows down, letting the scent of saltwater and Douglas fir roll through the cab of the truck.

The trip to the San Juan Islands had been too short. He would have stayed another week, but his clients were in a rush. A quick paddle to Orcas Island and then on to Lopez Island and Friday Harbor, paddling the short distance each day between islands and camping each night. He preferred kayaking alone. He preferred doing just about everything alone. However, his job as a backcountry guide with Ridgeline paid the bills. It was a necessary compromise.

Now, as he pulled off the highway and into the gravel lot of the Thurston County sheriff's office, his thoughts darkened.

He parked the truck, the engine still ticking in the quiet.

The vision had been so vivid.

The dead body.

The tattoo.

The red tin roof.

A dog barking.

He hadn't told anyone. Not even Lisa.

For eight years, Adam had been giving law enforcement agencies information about crimes he'd received in dreams and visions. Six days ago, he had met Detective Jordan Mitchell and explained what he had seen in the vision. Mitchell mentioned that they had a new unsolved murder—the killing of a woman named Rebecca Carlton. Detective Mitchell had just called and asked him to stop by the station.

Adam shut off the engine.

With a sigh, he stepped out of the truck. He ran a hand through his wavy brown hair as he checked his face in the rearview mirror. He'd fallen on moss-covered rocks the previous day, getting out of his kayak, and split his lip open. His hazel eyes scanned his reflection. The cut was already showing signs of healing.

He walked toward the building and pulled open the door to the sheriff's office. The buzz of conversation filled the room, punctuated by the occasional ring of a phone. Adam caught the eyes of a few officers and exchanged silent nods. Despite the acknowledgment, he felt the tension of being the outsider.

Adam approached Detective Mitchell, who sat at a cluttered desk surrounded by a fortress of case files and half-empty coffee cups. Mitchell looked up as Adam neared, his expression a mix of fatigue and relief. Mitchell's uniform was slightly rumpled, the shirt sleeves rolled up. He offered Adam a nod.

"Walker," Mitchell said, leaning back in his chair. "Thanks for coming. Have a seat."

Adam settled into the wooden chair opposite Mitchell, feeling the unease of being in a role he hadn't sought. He studied Mitchell's face, seeing the skepticism still lurking beneath the surface, tempered now by a grudging respect.

Mitchell shuffled some papers aside, clearing a space in the clutter. He tapped a manila folder in front of him. "We made an arrest."

Adam's eyebrows lifted slightly. "In the Carlton case?"

"Yep." Mitchell opened the folder, pulled out a photo, and slid it across the desk. "Name's Frank Eddinger. Ex-con, bounced around construction gigs. We picked him up last night."

Adam studied the photo. It was the man he'd seen in the vision. His confirmation couldn't be used as evidence, so he kept it to himself. Adam looked up from the photo. "You think he did it?"

Mitchell's mouth twisted. "We're pretty sure. Found a bloody jacket in the back of his truck, and a knife with a partial print that matches him. He's not talking, but the evidence is convincing."

"So, what I told you was helpful?"

Mitchell nodded slowly. "Yeah. That's the thing." He scratched the back of his neck. "You said to look for someone with a snake tattoo on the left side of their neck. Said he'd be hiding in a place with a red tin roof. Damned if we didn't find Eddinger holed up in an old house out past the quarry. Red roof, just like you said. He even has the tattoo."

Adam sat in the chair quietly.

Mitchell sighed and took a long drink from his lukewarm coffee. "When you first came in here, I thought you were full of it. Psychic powers? Come on. I kept your notes, but I wrote you off as a crackpot. But now..." Mitchell shook his head. "Now I don't know what to think. You gave us the tattoo. The roof. Even the dog barking near the scene —that was in your notes, too. And it all led us to him." He leaned forward. "So how does it work, exactly? Do you see it like a movie in your head?"

Adam smiled uncomfortably. "It varies. Sometimes, it's a dream. Other times, it's a single image or several of them. Sometimes it's clear. Most times it isn't." Adam looked at the detective. "You still think I'm crazy?"

"I think," Mitchell said, staring at the photo on his desk, "that crazy people don't solve murder cases."

Adam nodded and slowly got up from his chair. "Was there anything else? I need to go."

The deputy rose from his chair. "No, just giving you the update. Thanks for your help. If you get any more of those visions, you have my number."

THREE

SIX DAYS LATER.

Looking downward from the summit of Mount Rainier, the rocky spine of Disappointment Cleaver sat between the Emmons and Ingraham glaciers like a thin wedge of chocolate cake resting on a layer of buttercream frosting. Above the rocks of the cleaver, closer to the summit, glaciers turned into seracs—massive vertical slabs of ice weighing hundreds of tons each. Lower on the mountain, a snowfield stretched wide and glistening beneath the morning sun.

Adam guided a couple of roped hikers eastward across the snowfield toward a section of terrain known as the Ice Box—a glacial basin littered with broken slabs of ice, some the size of houses, others cracked and poised for collapse. "No stopping," Adam yelled from the rear. "Watch for falling ice. Move quick and keep the rope loose."

Jennifer moved with care, keeping a lookout uphill for signs of danger. Mark followed, holding his axe a little tighter than needed. A muffled groan echoed from somewhere above.

They emerged from the Ice Box and moved toward the Bowling Alley

—a sloping traverse strewn with rocks and debris that had fallen from the cliffs of the Disappointment Cleaver above them.

"Now it's falling rocks you need to worry about," Adam said. As they hurried across the dirty slope, a rock the size of a basketball careened down the mountain twenty yards behind them. "That's your warning shot," Adam said, "let's hustle."

They reached the base of Disappointment Cleaver, where snow gave way to steep, broken rock.

As they ascended Cathedral Gap, Adam instructed his clients to make adjustments. "Shorten the rope. There's no danger of falling into a crevasse here. The boulders we just dodged are caused by lazy people dragging their ropes and knocking them loose. Once we hit snow again, we'll increase our distance."

Mark nodded, adjusting his knot and securing the slack in the rope.

They ascended the ribbon of stone slowly, using their axes less for traction and more for balance on the loose volcanic ridge. The wind picked up. To the north, the Emmons Glacier shimmered like a cracked pane of glass. To the south, the Ingraham Glacier fell away in a broken, dirty sheet of blue.

At the top of the cleaver, they reached a flat saddle where other teams were resting. The trio removed their packs and found a place to sit. Adam ate a granola bar between gulps of water. Mark and Jennifer took photographs as they ate. When they were rested, Adam explained their options.

"We're at the decision point," he said. "From here, it's crevasses, snow bridges, and ladders, and the route is steep. We can turn back. There's no shame in that. Or we can push for the summit."

Jennifer sat beside her pack, sipping water, but said nothing.

Mark looked at her, then at Adam. "You think we've got the weather window?"

Adam stared up the mountain. The summit was rimmed with clouds that hadn't been there ten minutes ago.

"If we move now. But the bigger question is whether you're tired. Because it only gets harder."

Jennifer looked at Mark and smiled. "I'm in."

"Me, too," Mark said.

"Then let's rope up," Adam said. They stood, shouldered their packs, and adjusted the safety rope. "From here to the summit, stay at least 25 feet behind the person in front of you." Jennifer and Mark adjusted their tie-in point on the safety rope.

The upper mountain was a blanket of white without a patch of ground in sight. The trail climbed steeply on ridges of snow and ice. Crevasses along the route were bridged by shelves of snow that sagged ominously. They crossed over wider chasms on aluminum ladders laid flat and lashed together with ropes.

Jennifer led the party. At the next bridge—a compacted block of wind-hardened snow—Adam paused.

"Go slow here, Jen," he said. "Test it before you commit."

Jennifer took a cautious step. The shelf beneath her collapsed. She screamed and disappeared into the crevasse below.

The safety rope went taught, jerking Mark off balance and flinging him on his back.

"Arrest! Arrest! Arrest!" Adam yelled. He looked to see Mark flailing on his back. "Damn it, Mark! Get on your face and anchor yourself!"

The weight of Jennifer's body dragged Mark toward the precipice. He flipped onto his stomach and dug his axe and crampons into the snow. His movement finally halted. Shaken, Mark yelled to his fiancée. "Jennifer!"

"I'm here!" Her voice echoed from below. "I'm okay—I think!" Jennifer dangled in the crevasse fifteen feet below him. Mark pulled a stake from his pack and hammered it into the snow—the first step in setting an anchor to avoid being dragged into the chasm.

"You're doing fine," Adam said to Mark calmly. "I've got you. Once you have the anchor set up, transfer Jennifer's weight to it." Mark worked quickly, pounding the stake into the snow and testing to make sure it would hold.

Jennifer yelled again. "Hurry—I can't move!"

"I've got you!" Mark called to her.

Adam heard a deep rumble. The shelf beneath Mark fractured and collapsed, sending him into the crevasse. The rope jerked Adam violently under the weight of Mark and Jennifer's falling bodies. He dug his axe and crampons deeper into the snow, but it was useless. He was being dragged toward a meeting with death.

No anchor.

No time.

If he continued holding their weight, he would be dragged into the crevasse and die. The other option was cutting the safety line and letting them die. With his free hand, he pulled a knife from its sheath on his hip and opened the blade. The weight of Jennifer and Mark drew him closer to the edge.

He bit his lip and cut the safety line.

The end of the rope slithered into the abyss.

Jennifer screamed from the depths of the crevasse.

FOUR

THREE DAYS LATER.

The world was slowly reemerging for Adam, but it came back in fragments. A pulse oximetry monitor was clipped to his finger. A soft beeping interrupted the tomb-like silence. Electrodes were stuck to his chest with the attached leads connected to a transmitter in the pocket of his gown. An IV was taped in place on his arm. Adam closed his eyes, trying to evade the fluorescent fog that floated just above him.

A red-haired nurse in her mid-forties noticed his eyes flutter and stepped quietly to the bedside. "Good morning, Mr. Walker," she said. "Welcome to ICU. My name is Veronica."

Adam glanced at her but didn't respond.

Veronica checked the IV line and noted his vitals. "Are you feeling any pain?"

Adam turned his head and looked at the wall.

"You're scheduled to meet with one of our crisis counselors this afternoon. I think you'll like her."

Adam closed his eyes, disappointed. He was supposed to be dead. That was the plan. But things seldom went as he had planned.

"You're not being discharged today," Veronica continued gently. "But you'll be okay."

Veronica reached into her pocket and pulled out a folded piece of paper. "Your friend came by. She had to leave for work but asked me to give you this."

Adam lay there motionless, unwilling to acknowledge Veronica's kindness. Doing so would suggest there was a reason to cheer up, and he had decided he would continue sulking. He had, after all, just killed two people, though not out of malice.

Veronica sensed her presence was not welcome. She set the note on the tray beside the bed and stepped out of the room.

Later that afternoon, the attending physician entered, wearing a white coat and holding a clipboard. He didn't bother making eye contact. He was all business.

"Mr. Walker, you seem to be out of the woods. Your labs look good. No organ damage from the dosage you took. Luckily." He flipped a page. "I see you have no history of previous attempts to harm yourself, but we'll need to keep you here for seventy-two hours under psychiatric observation. Standard protocol."

The doctor waited for a reply. After several minutes without a response, he gave up. "We'll talk more tomorrow." He left the room quickly.

Adam turned his head toward the tray beside the bed. The note sat unfolded. A handwritten message was visible through the thin, backlit paper.

If you need anything, I'm here.
—Lisa

He lay still, the IV ticking with its slow drip. Emptiness began to fill the room. And when the room had received all the emptiness it could hold, it filled Adam as well.

FIVE

ADAM'S LOSS of confidence didn't happen all at once. Rather, there was a gradual erosion of certainty. Before the tragedy on the Ingraham Glacier, the signs were there. Whispers of doubt followed him like snowmelt slipping beneath a glacier—unseen, but steadily dissolving the foundations upon which he had built his life.

There was the incident at Devil's Lake. It was a routine day. Adam led a rock-climbing trip at a popular spot. He had set up a rappel anchor on Wiessner Wall with a length of nylon webbing, something he could've done blindfolded. Tie an overhand knot in one end of the webbing and pass the other end back through in the opposite direction to make a water knot. But that day, distracted or overconfident—he wasn't sure which—he'd tied a simple overhand knot, creating an open loop. If he had gone over the edge, he would have died, but he double-checked the knot and saw the mistake. Though he didn't show it outwardly, the realization terrified him. He'd laughed it off later with the others, but he didn't sleep that night.

Then there was the hike in the Cascades. He was guiding a four-day trek with a mixed-experience group. Fog and overcast skies had made shadow orientation useless. Still, Adam had chosen the wrong trail, leading them six hours off course. It wasn't catastrophic—no one was hurt, and the detour only added a few miles to aching feet. But Adam knew the truth: he had not been paying attention. His mind had been somewhere else, and when the trail forked, he didn't realize it. He could still hear the way the youngest client—a teenage girl with blisters on both heels—had tried not to cry. He apologized profusely. But the shame didn't pass.

Another time, during an exercise with Ridgeline coworkers, Adam swore he'd locked his carabiner gate. But the gate came under tension mid-climb, and his movement forced it open. The harness held him. The belay system caught. But it could've been different. Afterward, no one blamed him. Mistakes happen. Minds drift. But Adam couldn't stop thinking about how sure he'd been. And how wrong he was.

He began to wonder—occasionally at first, then constantly—if he'd lost his edge. An instinctive sharpness seemed to have ebbed away. Navigating the backcountry and performing high-risk maneuvers required more than strength. It required clarity of mind, the ability to assess risks and conditions, to decide the best course, and to act without hesitation.

But hesitation had crept in like fog. Quiet and pervasive. And then came the Ingraham Glacier. After that, there were no more justifications.

The office was quiet when Adam arrived. Muted mountain light filtered through the wide windows, casting pale golden rays across the hardwood floors and worn leather chairs. On the walls hung framed photos of past expeditions—summits conquered, smiles caught mid-victory, arms raised against the sky. Adam didn't look at them. He stood just inside the door, his hands tucked into his jacket pockets.

Across the room, Derrick Holden, owner of Ridgeline Wilderness Guides, looked up from behind his desk. His face was weathered from years of sun and wind, but today, it looked heavier than usual. "Adam," Derrick said, rising from his chair. "Come in. Sit." Adam crossed the room and took a seat opposite him. "You've already submitted your report," Derrick said, sitting again. "This isn't about paperwork."

Adam nodded, but did not speak.

"I asked you to come in because..." Derrick paused, searching for the right words. "Because I didn't want this to end in silence. And because I wanted you to hear this directly from me." He folded his hands on the desk. "No one blames you. Not me. Not the board. You followed every protocol. It was a freak collapse. No guide could have foreseen it."

Adam closed his eyes and let out a sigh.

"You did everything right," Derrick added. "I mean that."

A long silence followed. Outside the office, the muted whistle of wind moved through the pines. In another room, a creaking floorboard settled with a soft groan. Then Adam spoke. "I still see them," he said quietly. "Every night. I run the route again. I replay every decision. Every pause. Every rope check. I hear them shouting as the ice came down. I was the last one. I should've..." He trailed off.

Derrick shook his head. "That kind of thinking will break you, Adam." Derrick, ever the professional, knew Adam had already been broken, but out of respect, softened his prognosis.

Adam, having no need for subterfuge, got to the point of the matter. "I'm leaving," he said. "I'm stepping away. From guiding. From Ridgeline. From all of it."

Derrick blinked, stunned. "Adam—"

"I know it's sudden. But I can't keep pretending everything is okay. Just the thought of putting on a harness scares the hell out of me."

"Take time off," Derrick said. "A season. A year, even. But don't walk away for good. You have a gift. You belong out there."

"I used to think so, too." Adam said, staring at the thumbnail of his left hand. It had been bruised holding his position with his left hand while cutting the safety line with his right hand.

"I won't talk you out of it if your mind's made up. But I want you to know—you have a place here. If you ever decide to come back."

Adam stood, suddenly needing to leave. "I appreciate that," he said. "More than you know." He turned toward the door. He walked to his truck in the shadow of the mountains—cold, immense, and indifferent—mountains he had determined he would never climb again.

SIX

ADAM TURNED into the narrow driveway of Mountain View Self Storage. The sun had already dipped behind the ridge, and the sky had dimmed to a soft blue-gray as the moon began its ascent. The rows of identical metal doors reflected the remaining light, their surfaces dull and impersonal. He pulled up to unit 42-B, shut the engine off, and sat momentarily without moving.

This was the last stop.

His apartment lease had run out, and with it, the current chapter of his life had run its course. No more furniture to move. No keys to hand over. Everything he hadn't sold, donated, or thrown away was already in the storage unit or packed in dusty boxes and plastic bins in the back of his truck. He hadn't told anyone he was leaving. What would he say?

I'm sorry I failed.

I need to disappear for a while.

Hope you understand.

He stepped out of the truck and unlocked the roll-up door. It screeched as it rose, revealing a small, dim space lit only by the last rays of twilight. A kayak rested against the back wall. He picked up the nearest box from the truck—a crate of old board games—and carried it inside. After a moment of consideration, he placed it on top of a box labeled *Star Wars Collectibles*. That one had been hard to seal—full of childhood memories, convention finds, and a few things he'd convinced himself would be worth something someday. He stood there a moment longer, surveying the growing pile of memories reduced to cardboard and tape.

He returned to the truck. The amplifier came next. Heavy, unwieldy. He wrestled it out of the truck and into the unit, wedging it carefully between a stack of boxes and a milk crate full of vinyl records. He had pawned his last guitar to pay rent.

Out of the truck came plastic bins, boxes of photos, DVDs, and winter clothes. Last came the sealed cardboard tube containing a poster from the film *Tombstone*, autographed by the entire cast. Kilmer. Russell. Paxton. Elliot. It was a gift from his brother. He had always meant to frame it.

He laid it gently beside the amplifier, adjusting it so it wouldn't roll. The unit was small, but it held the essence of a life suspended. His phone buzzed. He pulled it from his pocket, expecting a calendar reminder or a spam call. Instead, he found a message from an unknown number.

> Hi, Adam. I was referred to you by a mutual friend who thought your expertise would make you a good candidate for a position I need to fill. The position is a wilderness explorer for a scientific research project that will document the behavior of a previously unknown species. The ideal candidate must be comfortable working alone. The research will be conducted in an exotic location. All expenses, including training, food, lodging, and air travel, will be paid for by the program, which is federally funded. The position requires a one-year commitment. If you're willing to join our team, please reply "yes."

Adam stared at the screen.

A year.

An exotic location.

A reason to disappear.

He wasn't interested in being responsible for the safety of others. *But if I'm on my own*, he thought, *that's a different story.*

He stepped out of the storage unit and looked up at the rising moon—full and shining, like a new penny. The light painted the gravel lot in soft gold. The whole scene felt surreal.

Well, he thought. *If I accept the job, I won't have to find another apartment. And maybe I'll get to visit the tropics on the government's dime.*

He typed a single word.

> Yes.

A few minutes later, the reply came.

> We'll be in touch with you soon.

Adam looked around the unit one last time. He pulled the door closed and slid the bolt shut. The padlock clicked into place with finality. He climbed into the truck, started the engine, and rolled slowly toward the exit. Behind him, the unit stood silent. The past, boxed and filed away.

SEVEN

ADAM SAT in a chair near the patio door. He glanced out the window at Mount Rainer, then looked away. Lisa's apartment was filled with rich mahogany and seafoam greens. Sophisticated. Stable. He looked at his girlfriend from across the table. "I got my stuff moved into the storage unit this evening."

Lisa was perceptive. Cheerful but not a cheerleader. Her green eyes looked at Adam lovingly. She had noticed changes. He was less talkative. He no longer dreamed about the future. The spark was gone. Mr. Walker had officially notified the world he was withdrawing from the game of life. But the game of life went on anyway.

Lisa looked down, then glanced at Adam through a veil of shoulder-length black hair. "Have you found another apartment yet?"

"No."

"Where are you staying tomorrow night?"

"At a cabin."

"Adam, you just quit your job, and I understand why you did that, but you have no income. And now your lease is up, and you have nowhere to live. I know you're going through hell, but this isn't how responsible adults act. Why don't you move in with me until you find a new place?"

Adam shook his head. "The last thing I want is to feel like a burden to somebody. And who said I want to be a responsible adult?"

"There's nothing wrong with being carefree and avoiding responsibility when you're young. But life is supposed to change you. You're supposed to grow up. Settle down. Get a job, buy a house... maybe have some kids."

Adam stared at the tabletop. "Did it ever occur to you that I don't want to be a suit-and-tie wearing, obedient member of society who attends school board meetings, follows the HOA rules, and colors inside the lines? What if I don't want to change?"

Lisa sighed. "It's not like you have a choice. Life forces everyone to change. It's called *growing*. Some people change for the better. Some for the worse." She paused, reaching for his hand. "You're a great guy. You have so much potential. I know you've been through a lot of crap. But I have to ask... what are you afraid of?"

"When I go out in the back country," Adam explained, "I have choices. If it's snowing, I can snowboard. If it's cloudy and cool, I can hike. If it's sunny and warm, I can go for a paddle. If it's raining, I might spend some time in the hot tub. There's plan a, plan b, and plan c. But when you get married, there's only plan a. There is no plan b." He shifted in his chair, his eyes meeting hers before continuing.

"What happens if we get married, have kids, and years later, I hate my job, our kids are growing up to be criminals, and trying to keep them out of jail is driving me crazy? In my mind, marriage is a lifelong commitment with no escape route. So, I end up stuck in a miserable life that I can't get out of."

Lisa returned his gaze with unbroken resolve. "That's a bit harsh. Marriage is what you make of it. If you choose to be good to the other person, they'll treat you with kindness. It doesn't have to be a chore. And if you raise your kids with the right values, they're not going to become criminals."

Her voice softened, "I would never expect you to color inside the lines, and I love the way you think outside the box. I never want you to lose that."

"That's what you say now. But you said life changes you. If that's true, how do I know in ten years you won't change into a woman I despise? I'm not ready to bet everything on an unknown future—"

Lisa winced at the remark. "Well, I highly doubt that I will become someone you *despise*, Adam. But the future is always unknown. Well... except for those dreams of yours. But you know what I mean. No one knows what will happen ten years from now. That's what makes life exciting. That's why you go out on your adventures, isn't it? The thrill of the unknown?" She ran her fingers through her hair. "Speaking of unknown futures, what's your plan for the next month? Since you rejected my offer, tomorrow, you're homeless. Aren't you concerned about stepping into an unknown future?"

"I'm moving."

"Moving? To where?"

"I'm not sure. I was contacted by someone who recruited me to conduct field research on a fully funded, one-year project. They didn't say where the job is located. So, there's no point in signing another lease. Until the job starts, I'll be staying in a rented cabin."

"Wait—you took a job and don't know where it's located, who you're working for, or when it begins?"

"That about sums it up."

"So, you've made a long-term commitment to something I didn't know about?"

"Life is full of surprises."

"Did it occur to you that I might want to have a say in this decision?"

"That thought did cross my mind."

"So, you knew I would object, but you accepted the job anyway."

"That's one way to look at it."

"And what about us? What does our future look like?"

Adam hesitated; the words were like cotton in his mouth. "I'm not sure. I love you, Lisa. Hell, you're the best thing that ever happened to me. But you want to get married, and I'm not ready for that. Maybe you should find someone who can give you what you want."

"What? I don't want anyone else. I want you." Tears formed in her eyes. "Did you take this job because it would give you a reason to break up with me?"

Adam didn't speak. He didn't want to cause more damage. Not to her. Not to anyone. His destruction was aimed inward. After a moment, he lifted himself from his chair and headed toward the door. With a lump in his throat, he closed the door softly behind him. Soft sobs escaped from under the door as he walked to his truck.

EIGHT

ADAM SHIFTED UNCOMFORTABLY on the narrow bed in the cabin, his gaze fixed upward, locked onto a web of hairline fractures within the wooded boards that branched across the barren ceiling like tributaries of a lifeless river. With each slow breath, dust motes danced in the fading shaft of light trickling in from a small window, indifferent to the storm raging silently within him.

His attention drifted downward, landing upon the half-empty whiskey bottle on its side by the bed, a temporary companion in his self-imposed exile. The label was smudged, the once-golden liquid betraying the passage of time through its depleted volume. Adam's hand reached out, his fingers wrapped around the cool glass. The cap yielded with a twist. He tilted the bottle back, letting the liquid fire cascade into his mouth. It was a welcome pain, a distraction from the relentless drumbeat of his battle-weary mind that continually drifted into the ether of what-ifs and might-have-beens.

Adam's gaze swept across the dingy confines of the cabin. The dim glow from a solitary bulb cast long, desperate fingers over the collage of wrinkled drawings that lay strewn like fallen leaves, an origami of dreams now irrelevant.

In his mind, a broken compass appeared, no longer able to point the way forward. It was a cruel parody of his current state—adrift and directionless, the magnetic north of his purpose obscured by doubt, guilt, and regret.

Adam took another swig from the whiskey bottle. The burn was less pronounced now, his senses dulled by the alcohol coursing through his blood. As the warmth spread through his chest, he found himself drawn to the window. He rose from the bed, his legs staggered as they made their way to the glass. He peered through the grimy pane into the night.

The city lights below flickered like a distant constellation, a civilization pulsating with life that seemed both achingly near and hopelessly far. Each twinkle was a story, a heartbeat, a connection he had once been part of but now observed as if from another planet. The isolation pressed in on him with the weight of a black hole, pulling at the frayed edges of his mind.

He turned back from the window, the city's luminescence casting ghostly shadows across his back. Adam's eyelids became leaden, his body a vessel drained of resilience. He stumbled back over to the bed and surrendered to gravity. The dim light blurred into a patchwork of shadows, and Adam fell asleep.

The solitude that cradled his descent into unconsciousness was disturbed when the door to the cabin opened silently. Four silhouettes stood framed by the doorway. The intruders advanced stealthily, their movements precise as a well-rehearsed play, the worn carpet muffling their footsteps. They encircled the bed where Adam lay, unmoving and oblivious. The men had come prepared to abduct him by force, using a gag and handcuffs, but the whiskey deemed these items unnecessary. Each man positioned himself at a corner, and on the lead man's signal, lifted the sheet under Adam, slowly. With his body suspended, they stepped in unison toward the door, and once outside, hoisted him into the back of a waiting truck.

NINE

ADAM'S EYES opened slowly to the embrace of a thin cot that cradled him. The ceiling above him was a seamless sheet of dull metal, reflecting back a faint, hazy image of his bearded face—a beard he had never had before. He lay there for a moment, confused and anxious, before slowly pushing himself up to a sitting position.

He moved gingerly as though even the act of sitting might trigger something unwelcome. A wince flickered across his face, though whether from physical pain or emotional trauma was unclear. Adam scanned the tiny room, his breathing the only sound punctuating the absolute silence. He appeared out of place against the sterile backdrop—a rugged figure of lean muscle, now confined within a perimeter of cold metal walls.

What the actual hell?

The room was stark, almost aggressively so. A spartan bed, presently occupied by Adam, hung from bolts affixed to a wall. On the opposite wall, there was a row of metal lockers. He got up to inspect them. They were not a permanent part of the room, he decided. They had been bolted into place as if for a special purpose. There were twelve lockers in all—each one numbered and devoid of handles. As he approached, two of the lockers clicked and the doors swung open. Adam peered into the first locker and found a stack of neatly folded gray garments identical to the shirt and cargo pants he was already wearing. Beneath them, he found a bundle of clean towels, socks, underwear, and what looked like thermal underlayers.

Nestled at the bottom of the locker, there were a pair of hiking boots and a pair of rock-climbing shoes. The same brand and size he had always worn.

They were new.

Inside locker two, he found two bars of soap in sealed wrappers, a metal box containing razors, a toothbrush, and a tube of unmarked paste. Beside them was a cloth pouch that held a set of grooming tools. Below them was a laundry bag.

The room was illuminated by four small lights embedded in the ceiling, one near each corner. An air vent was seamlessly integrated into the ceiling as well. Though he did not see a camera, he assumed one was present somewhere. There could be no other explanation as to why the lockers opened on his motion.

A small room jutted out from one corner, its lines sharp and industrial. Adam investigated and saw that it was a bathroom, complete with a shower. It occurred to him that he had to pee. He opened the bathroom door and closed it. When he was through, he washed his hands in a tiny sink. As he did, he noticed a bandage on the bend of his left elbow. He tore it off and tossed it in an opening below the sink, which he assumed was for trash. He inspected the wound, which he thought resembled a puncture left by an IV catheter that had recently been removed. Then, he noticed the bruise on his left thumbnail was gone. That puzzled him, but not as much as the fact that his nails had not been trimmed in a long time.

How long have I been sleeping? He wondered. *Where am I, and how did I get here?*

He tried to recall the last thing he did.

Drinking whiskey at the cabin.

Did I black out?

Is this a prison?

Did I commit a crime?

He tried desperately to remember something, anything that might hint at what had happened. But answers eluded him.

Adam exited the bathroom and scanned the metallic box, looking for any door, window, or markings that might give him a clue as to where he was. On the wall opposite the bed, near the corner, there was a cleverly concealed recess. He walked over to inspect it. His fingers traced the outline of what appeared to be the edge of a door that ran from ceiling to floor, though he saw no hinges, knob, or handle. Where the alleged door met the wall, there was a seam where, he assumed, the door's edge ended. It was the only feature that hinted at an exit, a potential escape from the metallic cocoon.

The sound of bolts unlocking echoed off the metal walls, startling him. The door opened. Filled with uncertainty, he peered through the doorway and, seeing no one, entered the adjacent room.

Standing in what appeared to be a slightly larger metallic prison, Adam scratched his beard. The room had a metal desk and computer terminal along the left-hand wall, as well as a chair. The far wall ended at a short hallway where there was another door. The only features that caught his attention were three narrow, metal tracks machined into the floor running the length of the room. He had been inside military aircraft and thought the rails built into the floor resembled those used to secure cargo.

He walked over to the metal computer terminal atop the desk. He hesitated, unsure how to interact with it. His fingers hovered above the controls. To the right of the computer sat a pile of granola bars and four bottles of water. He grabbed a couple of bars and shoved them in the left thigh pocket of his pants and stowed a water bottle in the right pocket. He sat in the chair and typed on the keypad below the terminal, his touch tentative at first, then more insistent.

The machine remained unresponsive. Frustration gnawed at him as each attempt to communicate ended in silence. At last, he gave up, rose from the chair, and returned to the bedroom.

TEN

IN A BUILDING BURIED in the bowels of Washington, D.C., a meeting had been planned that concerned Adam's current activities, though he knew nothing about it.

The meeting facility blended into the steel and concrete structures of the urban complex surrounding the Capitol.

A black SUV approached the entrance and stopped at the first security gate. Guards emerged from a small outpost. A gloved hand extended a badge as the driver's window rolled down. With a nod from the lead guard, the gate creaked open, granting the vehicle passage.

After she had parked, Doctor Evelyn Clark, the program coordinator, stepped out of her vehicle. The facility—a network of buildings connected by corridors—stretched in every direction. Cameras tracked her every movement. Nothing here went unnoticed.

Evelyn, a short, athletic woman in her mid-forties with blonde hair, walked with haste, passed through the lobby doors and then quickly navigated a series of checkpoints. Each door required her badge to be scanned, the machinery confirming her identity before unlocking with a mechanical click.

Finally, she reached the last checkpoint, a vault-like door that sealed the inner sanctum. A biometric scan confirmed her clearance. A guard opened the door, revealing the sparsely decorated sensitive information facility. Doctor Clark, dressed in a navy pantsuit, stepped inside, and the door closed.

The Agency Director, Matthew Lohmeyer, a portly, balding man in his sixties, sat alone at a table in the secure conference room, where even whispers felt amplified by the pristine walls. Classified documents were spread out before him, each sheet describing some detail of the high-stakes mission. He leaned back in his chair, his eyes narrowing as he absorbed the information. His face showed both anticipation and concern. He rose to greet Doctor Clark, offered her a seat, and returned to his chair.

"I assume you have an update on the mission," he said.

Doctor Clark seated herself. "We've seen positive indicators, though it's still early in the process."

Lohmeyer nodded, his eyes betraying a hunger for more information. "And the team? What's your assessment of their readiness?"

"We've selected the best people available and procured the needed equipment. The team is proceeding with their training as we speak."

Doctor Clark paused, choosing her next words with care. "All indications are that the mission is on a path to success. However, there are many variables involved, and we need to ensure that all of them are accounted for."

"I assume then, that the situation remains... fluid?"

"Yes, sir. That's a good description. We're monitoring the program's evolution closely. A full report should be available in a week."

There was a moment of silence as Lohmeyer considered the update, both what was said and what was not. The news eased his concerns.

"I trust you'll keep me informed of any changes," Lohmeyer said, with a subtle note of persuasion in his voice.

"Absolutely," Clark replied. "We're committed to maintaining full oversight. If there are any changes, I'll let you know immediately."

"Thank you, you're dismissed." Lohmeyer replied.

With that, Doctor Clark stood. Lohmeyer remained seated and continued flipping through documents on the table.

Evelyn exited the room, retracing her steps through the labyrinth of checkpoints. She knew the mission to Opturius was a long shot. Success would ultimately hinge on whether she had recruited the right mountaineer.

ELEVEN

THE SUN HOVERED on the horizon. Inside, Adam lay on the narrow cot, his eyes searching for an undetected irregularity in the ceiling. He tried listening past the repetitive din of his own thoughts, searching for something that would break the oppressive silence. The recycled air carried the scent of machinery and loneliness, a sterile, lifeless environment—not the expanse of a mountain ridge or the endless flow of a whitewater river, but the cruel confines of a cleverly crafted cage. Adam's mind replayed memories of his last moments before he had become a prisoner. The smooth texture of climbing rope in his hands. The sun reflecting in Lisa's eyes. Waking up in the ICU. The trip to the storage unit. And finding himself here, a captive of someone else's intentions.

He shifted on the cot. Then, he heard a noise—a beep that came from the adjacent space. Adam stood up and walked through the door into the other room. His gaze locked onto the sleek, dormant computer terminal. The screen was black and uncommunicative. But then, as if responding to his scrutiny, it flickered to life. He watched as white text scrawled across the display.

Hello, Adam.

Adam sat in the chair, placed his hands on the keyboard, and began typing:

Where am I? Why am I here?

The screen blinked in response, a silent acknowledgment of his presence. He waited. The computer responded with the efficiency of a guillotine blade:

It was necessary to bring you here.

He felt the heat of anger rising, but it was tempered by a stubborn refusal to accept the words as truth. His fingers moved quickly, driven by defiance and desperation:

Where am I? Why am I here?

The reply was swift:

You were the most qualified person available who agreed to join our team.

He typed, his hands pounding against the keys with a force that matched the pounding in his head:

I never agreed to this.

The computer was relentless in its detachment:

Yes, you did. You responded to the text inviting you on an all-expenses-paid expedition to an exotic location.

Adam blinked as the connection began to sink in. He typed again:

How long have I been here?

There was no reply. He typed again:

Where am I?

No response.

Anger turned to rage. Adam made a fist and swung with all his might at the computer terminal. The monitor's Lexan screen left a bleeding gash on his knuckles, yet it remained unscathed. Wincing in pain and dripping blood on the floor, he got up and walked back to the bedroom. The door closed behind him.

TWELVE

THE AROMA of ham pulled Adam from his sleep. His mind shuffled through possible explanations for it. Perhaps he was dreaming. Maybe he was awake but hallucinating. His thoughts were interrupted by the sharp clack of unlocking bolts. He sat up slowly and listened. The door that led to the adjacent room slid open. He got up and stepped through the doorway into what he decided must be the dayroom of the two-room penitentiary.

On top of the desk, beside the computer console, was a plate of neatly arranged ham and eggs, along with a steaming cup of coffee. The sight was both comforting and unsettling, an unexpected touch of hospitality in an otherwise austere environment.

He approached slowly, his eyes scanning the room for any sign of movement, any indication that he wasn't alone. The chair scraped slightly as he slid it out, the sound echoing in the empty space. He sat down and reached for the coffee. The cup was warm in his hand, the steam curling up to meet him. He took a careful sip, savoring the taste even as he questioned the motives behind the gesture. He ignored the plate of food. His eyes followed the door he had entered through, watching it slide closed with a soft metallic click, leaving him once again confined and isolated.

The door on the far end of the room opened, and a man entered, carrying a tablet. The mission leader moved with precision, stopping a few feet from where Adam sat, and offered a curt nod. Adam took in the man's presence—the attentive stance, crisp uniform, and emotionless blue eyes beneath gray hair that was cut high and tight—a demeanor that spoke of authority and detachment. Adam set the coffee cup down.

"I apologize for the way you were treated, Mister Walker. My name is Trevor Harris," the mission leader announced, the words sounding flat and rehearsed. There was no regret in his tone, just a matter-of-fact acknowledgment of the situation.

Adam remained silent.

Harris continued, "The circumstances required immediate action."

"And what circumstances would those be?" Adam asked, his voice edged with skepticism.

Major Harris gestured toward the plate of food. "We had to bypass formal orientation," he explained, ignoring Adam's question. "You must be hungry."

Adam glanced at the plate, then back at Major Harris. He tore off a chunk of ham and placed it in his mouth. After he had chewed and swallowed it, he turned his attention back to Harris. "Where am I and why am I here?"

Harris met his gaze; a flicker of something like amusement alighted in his otherwise impassive eyes. "Here is what I can tell you about where you are and why you are here:

"You are on the planet Opturius, billions of miles from Earth. The technology that brought you here is classified. You now have more knowledge of America's space capability than any member of

Congress. You should feel honored." Harris paused for a moment, then continued, "The planet Opturius is slightly smaller than Earth in size, and less dense due to its higher composition of water. The planet's atmosphere is similar to Earth's. Opturius is the fourth planet in the Thianos solar system. Thianos is a red dwarf. By comparison, it is one tenth the mass of the Earth's sun and it emits a fraction of the energy."

Adam took a bite of eggs, seemingly unfazed.

Harris continued the briefing: "Unlike most space missions, this one was not planned years in advance. It came together quickly in response to a crisis, the nature of which I'm not at liberty to discuss at this time. Normally, a mission like this would be assigned to a scientific team with a ship outfitted for conducting research. At the time the mission was given a green light, ships designed for scientific research were not available, and officers trained for this type of work were assigned to other missions." Harris paused and nervously ran his fingers through his hair.

"I hate when that happens," Adam said sarcastically.

Harris looked Adam in the eyes. "This is not a scientific ship. Its primary function is military transport. The equipment required for the mission has been temporarily outfitted on this ship. I'm not a science officer. I was given basic scientific training before we departed and instructions related to a handful of science goals, but this is not primarily a science mission. I'm an intelligence specialist and this is an intelligence gathering operation. We'd like to collect specimens of biologic and geologic value while we're in the neighborhood, but those are secondary considerations. Our primary goal is determining if intelligent life exists on Opturius, and whether we can communicate with it. Here's the bottom line, Mister Walker: I'm not the best candidate to run a mission like this, and this ship is less than ideal for what we must do. You're not a trained astronaut. All those factors being considered, the odds of the mission succeeding are slim." Harris let out a sigh. "However, it's the opinion of my superiors that this team has the best chance of succeeding against the many forces working against us."

Adam looked at Major Harris. "Is this some kind of joke? Do you expect me to believe I'm on a space ship billions of miles from Earth on a super-secret classified mission?" He shook his head in disbelief. "Give me a break."

Major Harris pulled out the tablet, then scrolled and read from it. "When I sent you the text, I asked you to agree to be... 'a wilderness explorer for a scientific research project that will document the behavior of a previously unknown species. The ideal candidate must be comfortable working alone. The research will be conducted in an exotic location. All expenses, including training, food, lodging, and air travel will be paid for by the program, which is federally funded.'"

"Wait... *you* sent that text?"

"I did. And you gave me informed consent. Informed as in, I told you the mission's parameters, and you agreed to them. It's unfortunate that we had to bring you here by force, but there was no other way. Although you agreed to join the mission, you didn't know the full details, and you likely would not have come here voluntarily. In time, perhaps you'll understand why it was done this way."

Adam laughed in disbelief. "Of all the people you could have recruited to join your circus, why me?"

"With your strength and coordination, I figured you'd make an excellent clown."

"That's hilarious."

Harris sighed impatiently. "You know yourself better than anyone, Walker. Consider your skillset and knowledge. You can probably deduce why you were chosen. Of course, we can't force you to cooperate with the mission."

Adam considered his options. They were few. A scene played out in his mind. Wyatt Earp had asked Doc Holiday to travel to Prescott, Arizona, to settle a feud he had with an adversary. Adam got into character, rose from his seat, stepped toward Major Harris, and looked him in the eye.

"Well now, Wyatt—you've been naught but gracious and obligin' to me all these years. Why, it'd be downright unseemly of me to turn you away over such a triflin' favor." "I'll take that as a yes," Harris said.

"I'm not agreeing to anything," Adam said tersely.

"Suit yourself." Harris turned and walked through the door, leaving Adam to sit in silence, contemplating his predicament.

THIRTEEN

ADAM AWOKE to the quiet of the bedroom. The cold, metal walls were as he had remembered them, but his gaze was drawn to the door leading to the dayroom, through which a faint glow of red light was visible.

He got up from the bed, moved toward the door, and then peered into the dayroom. It, too, was as he had remembered it, except for a previously unnoticed door in the left-hand wall between him and the desk, which was now open to the outside. He stood staring momentarily at the alien world awash in crimson light. Apparently, Major Harris had not been playing a prank.

Adam stepped back into the bedroom, pulled his socks and boots on, and returned to the open doorway. He studied the terrain before taking a hesitant step down from the spacecraft onto the planet's surface. The ground beneath his feet was a patchwork of hard, uneven surfaces interspersed with clumps of unfamiliar vegetation. He took a deep breath. The air was thin and energizing.

I guess I don't need a space suit, he thought. The massive red sun Thianos hung above the horizon.

Adam walked slowly across the rugged ground and soon realized he was in a shallow canyon—its edges softly defined in the red haze. He paused near the canyon's edge and took in the landscape. In the distance, he saw a mountain range where dark, jagged silhouettes met the sky. Lifting his eyes, he was greeted by a large, pale, pink planet suspended midway between the horizon and the zenith. It was the same mountain range and planet he had seen in the dream.

His heart rate increased. He felt dizzy. His vision narrowed, and his hands trembled. He stumbled back a step. Panic gripped him. He turned around.

Back to the ship. Get back to the ship. Where is the damn ship?

The hatch was gone. The ship had cloaked and was camouflaged against the canyon wall.

He dropped to his knees, clawing at the dust, trying to orient himself. His hands found footprints—his own, freshly made. He traced them backward.

Follow them. Just follow them.

He crawled along the ground following his footprints until they ended. He reached out, and his hand felt something solid. The ship was there. He scrambled through the open hatch.

The door closed behind him.

Adam stumbled into the bedroom and collapsed onto the bed. He covered his face with his hands and breathed deeply, the air hissing through his fingers.

I wanted to disappear, He thought, *but this is a little overkill.*

FOURTEEN

MAJOR HARRIS STOOD in the dayroom. Adam sat at the desk. He didn't look up. "I stepped out yesterday."

"I know."

Adam gave a dry laugh. "I didn't go far. Maybe fifty yards."

"Still counts."

Adam nodded slowly, then looked up. His eyes were tired. "I saw the mountains. The whole range. Stretched out under that sky like they'd been watching me for a thousand years." He paused. "And I lost it."

Harris didn't speak.

"I couldn't breathe. Couldn't think. I turned around to get back to the hatch, but the ship was gone, and for a second, I thought…" He trailed off. "I thought I'd never find it again."

"But you did."

Adam shook his head. "You made a mistake bringing me here. I'm not who I used to be. I can't do this."

"You already took the first step. Now take another. I'll adjust the mission's expectations."

Adam glanced up. "Why me?" he asked. "Why not just send a drone swarm to collect your data? Why drag me here under false pretenses?"

Harris folded his hands. "Because if all we needed was terrain data, mineral scans, or tissue samples, we *would* have sent drones. Robots don't whine about being told to climb mountains. They don't argue over ethics." He paused. "But that's not the goal."

Adam tilted his head. "Then what is?"

"We're here to answer a question," Harris said. "One bigger than any scan or specimen can answer: *Is* there intelligence on this planet? Not just problem-solving skill or tool use, but true intelligence—awareness. Consciousness. Maybe even... spirituality."

Adam frowned. "Spirituality?"

"The kind of intelligence that wonders. That loves. That creates. That reaches beyond itself."

Adam leaned forward. "You dragged me across space because robots can't find God?"

Harris smiled briefly, then his stoic demeanor returned. "Machines can't recognize or interact with what they don't understand. A drone can catalog life but it can't discern meaning. It can't feel awe. It can't ask, 'Is this sacred?'" He paused. "But you can."

"That doesn't justify lying to me."

"No," Harris said. "It doesn't. But if we'd told you upfront what the mission required—what you'd face, what it might ask of you—would you have said yes?"

Adam didn't answer.

"You wouldn't have." Harris continued. "And we couldn't afford to lose someone like you."

Adam stood abruptly. "If I'm so special, then why are you treating me like this? You put me in a cage and want me to be grateful for the privilege?"

Harris didn't flinch. "I want you to understand why."

"There's no excuse for the way you've treated me."

"I accepted a lot of risk when I recruited you. I knew you were struggling emotionally, but I felt you were the right candidate. I knew you wouldn't volunteer if you knew the truth about the mission, so I had to lie to you. And I knew once you realized you'd been tricked, you'd be pissed off and lash out, so I confined you until your anger subsided, otherwise, you'd hurt someone. The plan was to get you past that... to get you to a place where you'd be willing to cooperate. Look, I don't enjoy this cat and mouse crap."

"You still haven't explained why you picked me. There are hundreds of people that are more qualified."

"There were many reasons why I should have excluded you from consideration. Not the least of which was the Ingraham Glacier accident. And what happened after."

Adam looked away.

"I read everything," Harris continued. "The coroner's report. The investigation notes. I know about the suicide attempt. About Lisa. And about the fallout."

"Then why the hell am I here?" Adam yelled. "You don't send a broken man into the field! Not unless you're trying to bury him."

"No," Harris said. "You're right about that. But you don't send a *hollow* man either. And that's what every other candidate was."

Harris reached for his tablet, pulled up a page, and slid it across the table. "I went through the dossiers. Thirty-six names. World-class climbers. The cream of the crop."

Adam picked up the tablet and flicked through the profiles.

"And every one of them was a sociopath," Harris added.

"Ramsden's a little odd," Adam said, looking at the tablet, "but he's not a sociopath."

Harris continued, "I ran psych profiles on all of them. These men and women could summit anything—but for one reason or another they didn't meet the mission profile."

He paused.

"You, on the other hand... you tried to take your own life after losing two clients. I don't admire that," Harris said gently. "But I understand it. You carry the weight of guilt. And that means, deep down, you still have a moral compass that works."

Adam's hands tightened around the tablet.

"I didn't need the best climber. I needed someone who would instinctively do the right thing when every temptation pointed the other way. Someone who would listen to a voice no one else hears. Who wouldn't lie to protect his ego. Who wouldn't exploit what he finds for personal gain. I don't just need muscle. I need someone with a conscience."

Adam looked down at the images on the screen. Cold smiles. Award photos. All the right gear. Perfect records. Empty eyes.

"I'm still messed up," he said.

"I know," Harris replied. "But at least you know you're broken. That's the only kind of man I would trust not to break this world."

"So, what happens now?" Adam asked.

"Well, Humpty Dumpty, that's up to you. We can try to put you back together. If we succeed, you can help us understand the secrets of Opturius. Or you can walk away, and we both lose something we may never get back."

Adam set the tablet down. "I'm still angry."

"I'd be worried if you weren't."

Adam gave a small, bitter laugh. "It seems I don't have a lot of choices."

"You can only play the hand you're dealt."

"What do you need from me?"

Harris looked at him with those cold blue eyes. "I need you to do what you do best. Hike the local area and make note of anything you find that's interesting."

"That doesn't sound like looking for God."

"You may find it more interesting than you expect."

They sat in silence. No handshake. Just a fragile, tentative agreement between two men viewing a difficult situation from different perspectives.

FIFTEEN

THE FOLLOWING MORNING, Adam sat at the desk in the dayroom, his posture one of resignation mixed with optimism. A few feet away stood Major Harris in a soldierly stance. "Ground rules first," Harris said, his voice emotionless and direct. "Initially, you'll explore the planet within a three-mile radius of the ship."

Adam nodded in compliance.

"Observe and catalogue any life forms," Harris continued, "mentally, at first. Later, you can bring back specimens. You will report your findings to me immediately upon your return. Minimize your impact as much as possible. You've heard it before—pack it in, pack it out. We're not here to change the planet."

"What about human waste?"

"Bury it."

"Any rules for self-defense?"

"Remember, we're here as visitors. Diplomacy is the top priority. Try to be peaceful."

Adam smirked. "That's assuming everything goes as planned. Which it never does."

A shadow of a smile graced Harris's mouth, an acknowledgment of Adam's stubborn realism. "Hence the restriction on non-native technology," he said. "Exceptions can be requested—only if justified and approved in advance."

"And you decide what's necessary?"

"Yes."

Tension grew between them, with the weight of unspoken arguments, the need to assert authority, and its requisite demand for compliance. Harris's steady gaze met Adam's thoughtful eyes, neither man willing to look away.

"What technology is allowed?" Adam asked.

"You'll need a communication device for emergencies," Harris said, returning to the measured pace of his briefing. "Along with a camera and a pack for collecting specimens."

"Sounds like a high school biology trip."

"You survived high school. You'll probably survive this." He handed over the communication device, camera, and pack. "The communication frequency is channel one. Push the button on the side to alert the ship and talk. The camera syncs with the computer. Upload your images when you file a written report."

Adam accepted the items and set them on the desk.

"Our data does not suggest a danger of radiation, but to be on the safe side, we need you to clip this monitor to your pack or jacket any time you're off the ship. Each time you return, we'll take a reading from it." Harris handed Adam a tiny device with a spring-loaded clamp.

"What about a compass? It sure would be handy for navigating. Everything on this planet is red. Can I use a flashlight?"

"Those are fine." Harris paused. "Although the atmosphere should be safe without the need for breathing apparatus, we have an environmental suit if you need it."

"What about telemetry?"

Harris picked up a wristwatch. "Glad you asked. You'll need to wear this. It records your vital signs and transmits them to the ship, as long as you're within line of sight. If you plan on exploring any caves, let me know in advance."

Adam took the watch from Harris and secured it to his wrist. "And what if I encounter the locals?"

"Initially, just observe, and report what you find. We'll make a determination as to interaction in each case based on the available data."

Adam's eyes met Harris's again. "You always play by the book?"

Harris paused momentarily. "To an outsider, the military chain of command may seem like a harsh master, but it's highly effective when we follow orders. When we don't, we have chaos. It's a tradeoff I'm willing to make."

Adam looked around the dayroom at the silent surfaces and mute corners. "You're definitely ready for this mission, Major. I'm just not sure if I am."

Harris challenged him. "Why?"

Adam opened his mouth, expecting the reasons to come forth.

But nothing came.

He sat there, looking at the gear. Excitement filled him, followed by fear. He closed his eyes and shook his head.

You're not risking anyone else's life. It's just you that will be dead.

He opened his eyes and looked toward the door that led outside. He released a sigh of resignation. "Okay, I'll give it a shot."

A twinge of joy washed across Harris's face, but it was gone in an instant. "We'll start tomorrow."

SIXTEEN

JUST ABOVE THE HORIZON, the sun cast crimson light across the plateau. Adam stepped outside for the second time.

The air was dry and still, laced with a metallic scent that hovered just above the soil. Behind him, the ship vanished—just as it had the first time. He didn't flinch. He took a slow breath, exhaled, and walked forward.

The shallow canyon that ringed the landing curved like a soft bowl pressed into the planet's surface. The earth beneath his boots was loose and fractured in places, webbed with fine crystal lines that caught the sunlight like veins of glass.

He passed the canyon's rim and kept walking. Every step beyond that invisible boundary felt heavier, not physically, but mentally. He crested a gentle rise and came to a stop. In the distance, he saw a rock outcropping. To his left, the mountain range loomed large. He ignored it and fixed his eyes on the rock formation and continued walking. A wave of grief swelled in his mind.

He took a step, then a few more, all the while fighting an onslaught of emotions. He tried to focus on his immediate surroundings. There were no tremors and no shortness of breath. His legs kept moving, but his mind was overwhelmed by guilt. Images came uninvited—faces, voices, hands reaching, slipping, disappearing beneath the ice.

He stopped walking and stood there, halfway to the rock outcropping, and wept, tears and snot running down his face.

Minutes passed, but he remained there, his broken and bleeding soul waiting for an ambulance that never came.

He followed his footprints in the opposite direction. The ship was still invisible, but he found it anyway.

Back in the dayroom, he sat at the desk, trembling. Harris sat in the other chair, silently scrolling on his tablet.

Adam's eyes were red. His face was raw. "I can't go back out there," he said at last.

Harris studied him briefly, then closed his tablet and stood. "I want you to see the medical team."

SEVENTEEN

THE LIGHTS in Harris's bunk room were dimmed to half power, casting soft shadows across the metal walls. Chief Medical Officer Kyle Casey stood with a tablet in hand. He wore a desert camouflage uniform with no rank insignia visible.

Harris looked at him. "So?" he asked.

Casey sighed, glanced at the tablet again, then set it down. "He's in bad shape, Major. That's the simple version."

"How bad?"

"Persistent dissociative withdrawal. Disrupted sleep. Acute physical symptoms under stress—sweating, tremors, constricted breathing. You've seen it."

"Panic attacks," Harris said.

"More than that." Casey's voice was firm. "He's not bouncing back. He's decompensating. Each time he goes out there, it gets worse. His system is fraying."

Harris leaned back against the bulkhead.

"I sedated him after the last episode," Casey continued. "He didn't resist. He didn't even speak. He just lay there staring at the ceiling."

"In your clinical opinion is there any chance he might... come out of it?"

"If this were Earth, I'd ground him. No further stressors, no mission-critical decisions, no climbs. I'd monitor him for a depressive spiral and place him on an involuntary psych hold if he continues to deteriorate."

"So, what you're telling me is—he's unfit."

"I'm telling you that whatever he's carrying, it's still breaking him. And it's not going to stop because the mountain needs him."

Harris looked at Casey. "If he can't finish the mission—who can?"

Casey shrugged. "There's no one else trained for this terrain. Not unless you think one of your nav officers is secretly a world-class alpinist."

Harris didn't answer. He knew the truth. There was no backup. No second team. If Adam failed, the mission failed.

"I can keep him stable. Give him meds and monitor him. But if you send him out again in this condition—he might come back in pieces. Or not at all."

"Apparently, I bet it all on a man who didn't have anything left to give."

Casey moved toward the door. "That's above my pay grade. But if you want my advice?"

Harris looked up.

"Don't push him. Let him come around on his own. If there's anything left in him—it'll show up."

EIGHTEEN

ADAM STIRRED. His body was heavily sedated, but his drowsy state enhanced his receptivity to dreams and visions. He opened his eyes slowly. Kyle Casey sat a few feet away, slouched in a chair beside Adam's bed, flipping through a digital log on a tablet. He hadn't slept.

Adam blinked. His gaze drifted. And the room shifted.

He wasn't in the bedroom anymore. He was on a lake. The sky was dark. The water churned. Rain fell. The wind howled. A small boat rocked on the surface of the water. A boy sat at the bow—twelve, maybe thirteen. He was terrified.

His father was in the water, grasping at the edge of the boat. The boy tried to grab his arm and help him back into the boat, but the current was strong, and the wind drove the boat away from him.

The man's hand slipped.

A final look escaped his father's eyes—panic, and love. And he went under the surface. The boy screamed for help, but no one came to his aid.

Adam opened his eyes. He was back in the bedroom.

Casey hadn't noticed. He was still reading. Adam's voice cut softly through the quiet. "You were twelve."

Casey blinked and looked up. "What?"

"You were twelve. Fishing with your dad. A storm rolled in faster than expected. He got caught under the hull."

Casey looked at Adam with his mouth open.

Adam stared straight ahead. "You tried to reach him. You screamed until your throat was hoarse. But you couldn't pull him out. You were just a kid."

Casey stood slowly, his face pale. "How the hell do you—?"

"You've carried it ever since," Adam said without emotion. "Every time someone dies in your arms, it takes you back to that lake. You think it was your fault. You think you should've done something."

He paused.

"But it wasn't your fault."

Tears streamed down Casey's face.

Adam said nothing more.

It took a while for Casey to catch his breath. He wiped his face with his hand and stared at the floor. Then, hoarsely: "How can you see into someone else's pain like that but not your own?"

The question hit Adam like a roadside bomb. As he pondered the paradox, something shifted in his mind. His perspective began to change regarding the death of Mark and Jennifer.

Casey sniffed away his tears. A thought impression landed on him so strongly that he could not help but speak it out loud. "The only thing holding you back is your refusal to forgive yourself."

It was the diagnosis of a disease and the remedy. Adam listened in silence.

"Sorry, I don't know where that came from," Casey confessed.

"I do." Adam closed his eyes. In his mind, he saw Jennifer and Mark standing in the snow, smiling. Jenifer hugged Adam. Mark shook his hand. They seemed at peace. In unison, they echoed Casey's words: "Forgive yourself."

NINETEEN

ADAM AWOKE with a new view of the mission. Casey was right. He had been holding himself back over guilt. He still felt sorrow when he thought about the incident on the Ingraham Glacier, but it no longer paralyzed him. He told Harris he wanted to take another stab at his assignment and Harris approved.

The airlock opened, and Adam stepped out of the ship. His boots met the mineral-crusted ground with a soft crunch, and for a moment, he stood there, motionless, small, and stunned by the immensity of what lay before him. A cherry-red sky stretched from horizon to horizon, streaked with ribbons of darker crimson pulsing slowly as if the planet itself breathed. Thianos loomed above, not merely a sun but a red giant —massive, brooding, and eternal. It drenched the world in a deep glow that swallowed all shadows, giving the landscape a dreamlike reality. Adam closed his eyes. The scent in the air was sharp and clean. It replaced the stale recycled air of the ship, filling his lungs with something real, something alien. His chest tightened—not from fear, but from the weight of a feeling he hadn't expected: reverence.

He thought that perhaps, if he grounded himself in a study of the flora and fauna, it would silence his emotions. He flipped the switch on his headlamp, its white light providing a more accurate assessment of color. The plateau beneath him shifted—translucent veins of violet and gold rippled through the cracked surface. He took a tentative step forward, knelt, and brushed his hand over the terrain. To his surprise, it responded. Tiny threads of bioluminescent moss recoiled from his touch, dimming briefly, then pulsing back to life. The colors reminded him of bruised fruit—violet, chartreuse, and oxidized copper.

Something skittered. Adam pivoted, his heart thumping. A creature no larger than a rabbit had darted from beneath a low-slung, fibrous plant that looked like a cross between a sea anemone and a tumbleweed. The animal was translucent, almost gelatinous, with a shell of iridescent plates that opened and closed in rhythm with its motion. It froze, pulsing in place as if probing him, then flickered out of sight with a sudden shimmer. Adam stared at the spot where it had vanished. "Camouflage. Great."

He felt out of place—an intruder in a cathedral not made for him, yet part of him welcomed the strangeness. A low ridge curved ahead, covered with what looked like crystalline growths. As he approached, they reacted—each stalk lifting slightly, rotating toward him like antennae. A soft chiming noise echoed from within the cluster, not mechanical, but organic—a resonant, melodic sound. He crouched again, speaking aloud though no one could hear him. "Are you talking to me?" There was no response—only the quiet, tonal shimmer, like wind chimes swaying in slow motion.

He pulled a compass from his jacket pocket. He knew he was not on Earth and that the compass needle would not indicate magnetic north. But, he reasoned, if there were a magnetic pole on Opturius, it would influence the needle's swing. Regardless of the magnetic pole's actual location, relative to that direction and the fixed position of the ship, he could navigate the local area. He began moving east, slowing or stopping occasionally to inspect insects, plants, and odd rocks. He placed several samples into his pack, though he didn't take the time to label or log them properly.

After half a mile, he spotted the rock outcropping in the distance, its jagged silhouette beckoning him to explore it. His heart rate increased with effort and anticipation as he made his way toward it. The ground rose and fell beneath his feet, an uneven terrain that hinted at geological upheavals. Adam felt a sense of connection to this strange land, reminiscent of places he'd visited on Earth, though nothing here was quite the same. Another half mile brought him to the base of the rock outcropping. He paused, studying the rugged formations that towered above him. Alien plant life clung to the crevices, their tendrils reaching out as if in silent communication with something unseen.

A narrow cleft passage cut through the rocks. Adam hesitated at the entrance, one boot lingering on sunlit stone. He exhaled slowly, steeling himself, then stepped into the cool shade. His footsteps echoed softly against the stone walls. He walked less than a minute before rounding a blind curve in the passageway. He stopped for a split second when an object came into view, then quickly jogged in the opposite direction out of fear. He was certain the thing had moved, and he didn't want to risk an attack. Back at the sunlit entrance, he caught his breath while observing the passageway for signs of movement.

What the fresh hell was that?

The light in the stone corridor was dim, and he had moved so quickly away from the object that he wasn't sure what he had seen. All he remembered was seeing something tall and dark that appeared to be moving.

He listened and decided that it was no longer moving—at least, not toward him. Slowly, he retraced his steps back into the darkened passageway. The blind curve came into view again. He stopped and looked to see if the object was still there. He saw nothing. He advanced until the curve was behind him. Still nothing. Whatever it was, it was no longer there.

Adam walked back in the direction from which he had come. The encounter had unnerved him. He wasn't certain the object he had seen was real. As the shallow canyon came back into view, the rock outcropping disappeared behind him. He found the trail of footprints, followed them to the ship, and went inside.

He went to the bathroom, grabbed a granola bar and a bottle of water, then sat at the desk and began entering his report into the computer. Major Harris walked over and stood behind him, reading the field report on the screen over his shoulder.

"You only logged six samples," Harris said quietly. "No tissue, no spores, no soil core. You were out almost three hours."

Adam glanced behind him. "I'm not done with the report," he said, irritated. He stopped typing and stared at the computer screen, uncertain of how to proceed.

"I saw something," he said at last.

Harris moved around and took the opposite chair. "What was it?"

"I was about a mile east of the ship, near a rock formation. There's a narrow passage through it. I decided to explore it. Five hundred feet into the passage, I turned a corner and—" He shook his head. "There was something there. Twelve, maybe fifteen feet tall. I didn't get a good look."

"What did it do?"

"I don't know. It scared the hell out of me and I took off running." He gave a short, embarrassed laugh. "I went back to see if it was still there, but it was gone."

"You sure it wasn't one of the taller flora forms?"

"I wouldn't take off running if it was a *flower*," he said, annoyed.

"Right." Harris said. "Well, you saw something, and that's enough for me. I'd like you to go back tomorrow and see if shows up again."

TWENTY

THE NEXT DAY, Adam headed east into the light of Thianos, and returned to the rock outcropping. He approached the passage between the rock walls cautiously, and walked until he came to the blind curve and stopped.

There it was. A dark column of stone was partly blocking the passageway. He had not imagined it.

It was tall—easily twelve feet—a natural mineral column formed by some strange geological process. Its surface was smooth and dark, spiraling subtly like a wind-sculpted stone. But even in the dim light of the passageway, it shimmered faintly—an inner glow was present, a soft bluish-green radiance, pulsing slowly in waves. It had no face, no limbs in any conventional sense. Its base flared slightly. There were no obvious sensory organs. It did not move. And yet—it *had* moved. When he first observed it the previous day, it was the movement that startled him.

How does a rock move? He wondered. Adam drew near the column cautiously, though he sensed no threat. It did not seem to acknowledge him as he approached.

He stood in silence, remembering Harris's instruction: *observe first.* He pulled the camera from his pocket and took a couple of pictures. He thought about trying to communicate—perhaps speaking aloud or attempting a simple gesture. Adam looked where he had seen light emitted a moment earlier. It was now dark.

"I mean you no harm," he said softly.

A pulse of blue light rippled across the being's surface, apparently in response to his greeting. Adam walked slowly around the column of stone. It remained stationary.

"What's your favorite Val Kilmer film?" he asked with a smile.

The light pulsed softly again, casting a glow on the canyon walls.

"Tombstone, huh? Me too."

Adam stared at the enigma before him, content for now to note the being's existence and report to Major Harris what he had found. He turned and walked toward the opening at the edge of the rock outcropping. With a final, lingering glance over his shoulder, he turned back toward the ship.

Adam retraced his steps across the rocky plateau, his thoughts a whirlwind of questions and possibilities. This time, rather than fear, the encounter had left him exhilarated. The calmness of the creature lingered in his mind—a puzzle he wanted to solve. Its response to him was strangely comforting.

The landscape stretched out before him as he moved westward. Bulbous plants nodded in the wind, their translucent leaves shimmering like ghostly flames.

As he neared the ship, anticipation built. He was eager to share what he had seen, to relay the strangeness and wonder to Major Harris.

The invisible ship waited for him in the recess of the canyon. He approached with a sense of resolve. At last, his footprints came to an end. He reached out his hand to confirm the ship was still there and made contact with its smooth surface. His hand located the doorway, and he climbed inside.

Adam had just finished entering his report in the computer when Major Harris stepped into the room and took a seat across from him. "Radiation sensor?"

Adam unclipped the sensor and slid it across the desk. Harris set it aside, then scrolled through pages on his tablet.

"I've reviewed your notes," he began. "According to your report, you observed a tall, columnar form, with no discernible sensory organs, some type of internal luminescence, and no signs of aggression. Is that still your read?"

Adam nodded. "Yes. I saw it shift its position when I first approached it yesterday. After that, it didn't move the entire time I was near it either today or yesterday. It seemed to be aware of me. I'm more certain of that now."

"You're saying it responded to your presence."

"Not with gestures or speech. But it didn't need to. Yesterday, it was moving and then halted when I approached. Today, I spoke to it and it seemed to respond."

"I saw the photos you uploaded. Your report says you noticed colored lights on its surface illuminating in response to your greeting."

"That's correct. It also responded when I asked its favorite Val Kilmer flick," Adam said, grinning.

Harris smiled. "Based on your report, it seems we have our first intelligent life form. We have protocols for this," he said. "Even on expeditions like this one, where we're technically off the map."

Harris slid the tablet across the desk. Adam's eyes scanned the text.

Harris continued: "There's a process for assigning provisional names to newly encountered sentient species. It's mostly for internal communication and records to keep the people back home happy." Harris turned the tablet back toward himself and read aloud: "In the event of first verified observation of a new sentient species, the field officer shall designate the species with a provisional identifier. The first assigned designation is to be: Zenolith."

Adam blinked. "That's prewritten?"

"Standard operating procedure. Some committee back on Earth thought it would make things easier. No need to debate over naming when you're in the field. It's just a placeholder."

"So, it's official?"

"It has a name. Until we have reason to call it something else."

Adam looked at Harris for a moment, then spoke: "I want to go back."

Harris met his eyes, still unsure about Adam's mental state. He'd done well today, but he didn't want to push him. "You'll get your chance. But there's more of the planet to be explored. Your notes say you traveled one mile east of the ship. Is that correct?"

"That's accurate as far as I can determine what direction east is."

"I read your note on that. I agree with your proposed methods for terrain navigation. As long as we have a couple of fixed points, all directions can be assigned relative to them. We know what lies east of the ship. Tomorrow, I'd like you to travel west and see what's out there." Harris paused, remembering what Casey had said. "If you feel up to it," he added.

Adam sat quietly and took an emotional inventory. "I felt good today. At least I didn't make a complete ass of myself. I think I'm ready."

Harris nodded. "If you need anything, let me know." He rose from his chair and exited the dayroom.

TWENTY-ONE

ADAM CLIMBED a ridge of cracked shale-like stone west of the ship before descending into a basin. The wind funneled through narrow gullies, stirring trails of dust into the air. Sparse vegetation gave way to fields of smooth stone, carved by ancient erosion into flat terraces and crescent-shaped ridges.

After half an hour of walking, he came to the highest point of a rise and froze. Not twenty yards ahead stood a Zenolith.

It hadn't been there a moment ago. He would have seen it. The last time he had seen one, it had remained silent, as far as he could tell. Present, and responsive, but passive. He entertained a new thought: *What if it wasn't just passively observing him? What if it was actively scanning him, as if he were an intruder?*

As soon as he had entertained that thought, a flood of images filled Adam's mind that were chaotic. He had seen visions in rapid succession before, but they always conveyed a coherent message. These did not.

Adam put the images out of his mind and looked at the Zenolith, focusing on one thought: *I want to understand.*

Suddenly, a pulse of light darted from the Zenolith's core—bright, almost blinding.

Adam closed his eyes.

A single image flashed into his mind. He saw a circle of black stones set in a spiral, each inscribed with marks that glowed like embers. At the center, there was an empty space. He had the impression it was not hollow, but rather, a place reserved.

The image vanished. Adam opened his eyes. He waited, staring at the Zenolith.

Then, the Zenolith sent another pulse.

This time, an image of a tree appeared in Adam's mind—alien in shape but unmistakably a tree—growing in a barren field. Its roots were spread wide, but instead of drawing water from the ground below, the roots seemed to absorb light funneled downward from a ring suspended in the sky. A beam of light connected the ring to the crown of the tree. Then, the image vanished.

The visions hadn't come with sound or sensation—just imagery. Crisp, full-color, hyperreal.

Adam crouched with his hand touching the ground and closed his eyes. *A circle. A tree. A source of light above. A center left empty. Maybe vacated.*

His mind worked to parse the images. Each one carried some meaning, but a meaning that was, for some reason, concealed. He'd have to unpack them one layer at a time. But first, a question hovered in his mind: *Could he answer the Zenolith?*

Adam stood slowly, looking at the column of living stone.

He concentrated, then formed a single image in his mind, visualizing it with as much clarity as he could muster: a snowcapped mountain, quiet and peaceful.

He focused his attention on the Zenolith. His intention was a willingness to share. For a long moment, the Zenolith did not respond.

Then, a ripple of blue-green light passed across its surface. It did not send another image, but Adam sensed it was an acknowledgment.

They had spoken.

Harris sat at the desk in the dayroom, nursing a cup of something that steamed but didn't smell like coffee.

Adam stood across from him, his arms folded.

"So," Harris said, gesturing for him to sit. "I read your report. You saw another one."

Adam nodded. "I did. A little over a mile west of the ship. This time, it communicated."

Harris straightened slightly in the chair, setting the cup down. "You're sure of that?"

"It didn't speak. In fact, it didn't make a sound. But I sensed it was sending images to my mind. They were random. I couldn't make sense of them at first. Then, I thought 'I want to understand.' Immediately, a pulse of light hit me. And then, I received more images, but they were clear. Like transmissions… or visual packets of data."

Harris echoed his words. "Visual data packets?"

"I only understood the visions that came after the pulse of light."

Harris thought about his words. "Chaos before the pulse then clarity after it. Do you think the pulse of light decoded them?"

Adam smiled. "I hadn't thought about it that way. You may be right."

"Describe the visions."

"There were two that I could see clearly, after the light." Adam closed his eyes, recalling the images. "The first was a ring of black stones arranged in a spiral. Each one had glowing marks etched into its surface, but at the center of the spiral was an empty space. It seemed like it was intentional, like the space was reserved for some purpose."

"You think it represents a location or a site?"

"Maybe. The second image was a tree—alien, but definitely a tree. It was growing in barren ground. Its roots didn't go deep—they flared outward. Above the tree, suspended in the sky, there was a glowing ring. A beam of light flowed from the ring into the crown of the tree, and the roots responded, not to water, but to the light."

Harris sat quietly, processing Adam's descriptions.

Adam continued. "I think the first image was a message about the Zenolith themselves. A kind of identity or structure maybe. The spiral of stones might represent them collectively—each one with an individual purpose—but with a shared center. I got the impression that they want the center to be filled."

"With what?"

Adam hesitated. "A revelation. A return of something missing. Or maybe... a catalyst."

"And the tree?"

"That one felt more personal. I think it was about growth. It seems to illustrate the idea that it doesn't come from below, but from above. Illumination feeding transformation. The land was barren. But the light from above made life possible. It might be a metaphor for our mission. Or for me personally. I'm not sure."

"You think it's symbolic only?"

"I don't see anything literal in it. But I'm open to possibilities."

"Did you respond?"

"I tried. I projected an image back—something that came to me in the moment. A snow-capped mountain. I think it worked."

"Worked how?"

"The Zenolith pulsed with light afterward. It seemed to be an acknowledgment. It didn't transmit an image back to me, but I felt like we connected."

Harris tapped a few notes on his tablet. "That's your third contact in as many days."

Adam smiled. "I suppose it is."

"You need to get ready for a fourth."

TWENTY-TWO

ADAM HEADED EAST across the plateau, the sky above him streaked with darker clouds. When he arrived at the rock outcropping, he moved quietly between the vertical walls. He stood in the narrow corridor for several minutes, listening to the wind hum through the stone arches, waiting for movement that didn't come. The place where he had previously encountered the Zenolith was now abandoned.

He sighed.

Not today.

With the shadows shifting northward, Adam left the passage between the rocks and turned south down a rocky slope, angling toward a low depression in the terrain. He followed it for about a mile, moving at a steady pace, his eyes sweeping the ridges ahead. The land here was broken, split by old fractures and studded with plants that trembled in the rising breeze.

Standing atop a shallow rise, tall and unwavering, was a Zenolith, its bluish-green glow pulsing faintly beneath its spiraled shell. The moment he saw it, Adam felt a gentle pull—an invisible tether drawing him forward.

He climbed the rise slowly. The wind whistled in low tones around the rock spire. The maroon light from above fractured as it passed through distant clouds, casting flickering shadows over the land.

As he approached the Zenolith, a pressure filled the air, like static before a storm. He stepped closer. He could feel the energy now. It reminded him of standing beside a massive engine—the sensation of power moving. As he drew closer, his foot struck a rock, causing him to pitch headfirst into the column of stone. He hit his head on it and lay bleeding on the ground at its base.

Adam opened his eyes, and the world shifted. He was no longer lying on a ridge beneath a red sky. He was inside a storm. The sky above him roared with noise, and light—dark clouds spun in chaotic spirals, alive with electricity. Lightning flashed in arcs across the heavens. The wind whipped with terrifying intensity, driving debris across the landscape at breakneck speed—shards of stone, broken limbs of alien plants, clods of red dirt hurled like missiles. And in the center of it all was the Zenolith. The being stood firm, unflinching in the midst of the chaos.

Adam watched from somewhere both near and far. He felt the grit of the sand and wind against his skin, heard the sharp whine of air forced through narrow passages, and saw the stones battering against the spiral column with brutal force. The ground trembled with each concussive strike. But the Zenolith did not move. Its glow remained steady—its form rooted.

Wind tore past.

Dust whipped in sheets.

Lightning struck nearby, casting the world in stark flashes of white.

Rocks bounced off its surface. Some exploded on impact, but it held its position, unmovable.

And then—suddenly, stillness. The wind ceased, and the clouds broke. The light of Thianos returned. The Zenolith remained unmarred, its light still pulsing gently.

Adam opened his eyes with a sharp breath. He was lying at the base of the Zenolith again, the wind tugging softly at his sleeves, the red sky calm above him. His pulse thundered in his ears, but the storm was gone. He sat up slowly. Every nerve in his body felt charged. He held his hand to his head and wiped a smear of blood from his forehead. He looked up at the being. It had not moved.

He didn't know if the vision had been a dream, a trance, or something else. But he knew what it meant. He rose to his feet and took one last look at the silent sentinel before turning back toward the ship.

Adam sat at the desk in the dayroom, nursing a welt above his right eyebrow, a dark line of dried blood visible along his temple. He held a wad of gauze against the injury. Major Harris entered and took one look at him. "Please tell me the other guy looks worse."

Adam didn't answer.

Harris sat down across from him, eyeing the injury. "Head wounds always bleed more. You'll survive."

"I hit a rock," Adam said, trying to diminish the fall.

"You fell into a monolithic alien life form," Harris corrected him. "Still counts as the most original way to injure yourself on this trip."

Adam smirked. "I'm just getting started." He lowered the dressing, revealing the bruised and swollen gash.

Harris stared at the wound, unimpressed. "Walk it off, sissy."

Adam shook his head. "You have the bedside manner of a cactus."

"I'm intelligence, not medical."

"I can see why."

Harris shifted the conversation. "So. You saw another one?"

Adam nodded. "South of the outcropping. A mile down into a broken ridge line."

"The first encounter was a mile east. The second was a mile west. This one was a mile south. So, what happened?"

Adam placed the dressing aside. "It was intense. I could feel something when I got close. There was a pressure and then I felt power. I felt drawn, so I walked toward it. Then I tripped on something and went down hard. Hit my head against the damn thing."

"That's one way to ring God's doorbell," Harris quipped. "Did you happen to see a burning bush?"

Adam gave a short laugh. "When I opened my eyes, I was somewhere else. Not the plateau. I was in a storm. It was massive. Violent. Like the sky was coming apart."

"A vision?"

"I don't know. Maybe. But it wasn't abstract. It was tactile. I could feel the wind. I could hear the debris hitting objects and taste the dust. The Zenolith was there."

"What did it do?"

"It was there in the center of the storm. Everything around it was chaos—shrapnel, lightning, thunder, wind—but it never flinched. It didn't fight it. It just... stood there."

"Sounds like a metaphor."

Adam smiled. "Winner winner... can I get a damn chicken dinner?"

"What, now you want a reward for smacking your head on a rock and hallucinating?"

"It's a *'monolithic alien lifeform,'* thank you very much. Seriously, Major, these granola bars are getting old. What else do you have to eat on this bucket of bolts?"

Harris sighed. "I'll see what I can do. Now, back to the vision."

"The vision with the Zenolith... I think it was a personal message."

"Based on..."

"What it knows about me."

"So, it read your mind and gave you a personal coaching session?"

"I know it sounds crazy, but that's what it felt like. I could be wrong. It wouldn't be the first time."

"Hell of a therapist, that thing." Harris scratched his chin. "You realize that if I put that in a report, they'll start speculating about telepathic intent and cross-species messaging."

"Maybe it was just a concussion," Adam said.

"I know I'll probably regret asking this, but what if it was... some kind of prophecy?"

"Be careful, Major. Next, you'll be telling me about your dreams."

Harris reached into his pocket, pulled out a bandage, and slid it across the table. "Patch yourself up, Walker. We've got more aliens to meet."

TWENTY-THREE

THE MORNING WAS dry and bright as Adam trekked across the plateau south of the ship. He wasn't searching for anything specific—just walking, watching, listening. He passed the usual scatter of prairie creatures: quick-legged insects that clicked when they ran, lichen-covered scavengers darting between stones, and bulbous, twitching plants that opened and closed like valves. The land, as always, was alive.

Then, something caught his eye. Perched atop a flat, sun-warmed boulder was a small reptilian creature, no larger than a ferret. Under the illumination of his flashlight, its scales shimmered in shifting metallic hues—turquoise to violet to rust, depending on how the light hit it. A translucent frill ran the length of its back, twitching faintly like a solar panel tracking the sun. Adam crouched, watching. The creature chirped softly. Adam mimicked the sound it had made with a click of his tongue. The creature answered, leaped in the air, did a forward somersault, and landed on all fours with a flourish. "Well," Adam said, "you're a performer."

He took out a power bar, broke off a piece, and tossed it onto the rock. The creature pounced, devoured it quickly, and then looked back at him, expectant. Over the next several hours, Adam stayed nearby, feeding it in increments and experimenting with gestures. He learned that by moving his hand horizontally and lowering it slowly, he could make the creature lie flat, its frill folding back as though preparing to sleep. Making a circular motion with his finger caused it to leap into the air and execute a full somersault. A raised palm caused it to freeze and tilt its head in exaggerated confusion.

Most interesting of all, it mimicked. Clicks, chirps, soft whistles—even the sound of Adam rubbing his hands together. The creature would reproduce the noise within seconds, then embellish it with flair. Its superpower, he decided, was mimicry.

He laughed out loud as it chirped out a sound uncannily similar to the zipper of his pack, then tried to unzip the side pocket with its tiny clawed hands. "You're absurd, a real jester." The name stuck.

Court Jester.

He knew the scientists would eventually slap a clinical binomial on it —*Opturisa mimetica* or some such nonsense—but to him, it was the Court Jester.

Then came the trick that sealed the deal. When Adam snapped his fingers, the creature froze instantly. Its frill lifted. Its head turned with laser focus toward the sound. Then, with a theatrical wind-up of its body, it launched a wad of saliva in the direction of the snap. The glob sailed several yards and landed with a wet *splat* against a nearby rock.

Adam stared. Then he laughed until he was breathless. "Well, Jester... we're going to have some fun."

That evening, he returned to the ship with Jester tucked securely into the top compartment of his pack. The creature remained still during the journey, only occasionally sticking its head out to survey the terrain, its frill rippling like a curtain in a breeze.

Inside the ship, the dayroom was quiet. Harris sat at the table, reading data off his tablet, a steaming mug of tea beside him. Adam strolled in and set his pack on the floor.

Harris glanced up. "Good hike?"

Adam grinned. "Productive." He unzipped the pack. The Court Jester leaped gracefully onto the table, landing with the softest *thump*. It posed dramatically, with its frill flared like a fan.

Harris nearly dropped his mug. "What in the name of Jehoshaphat?"

"This," Adam said proudly, "is the Court Jester."

"It's alive."

"It's brilliant," Adam replied.

Harris fumed. "You brought a God damn alien animal onto the ship without permission," Harris said, standing slowly. "That's a violation of safety protocols."

Adam raised a hand. "I thought we were here to examine alien life forms."

Harris stared at the creature, which was now preening itself with exaggerated flair. "Is it dangerous?"

"Only if you're allergic to comedy." Adam made a slow circular motion with his finger. Jester chirped, sprang into the air, performed a somersault, and landed with a theatrical bow.

Harris blinked. "You trained it to do that?"

"I've been busy." Adam moved his hand flat, then lowered it. Jester immediately flopped down, belly to the table, its limbs spread, its frill flattened like a pancake.

Harris couldn't help it—a smirk appeared on his face. "Alright. That's... impressive."

"Here," Adam said. "Your turn."

Harris raised an eyebrow but mimicked the circular gesture. Jester popped up and did a slightly crooked somersault before landing sideways, then chirped once and resumed grooming.

"Not bad," Adam said. "Now snap your fingers."

Harris frowned. "What for?"

"Just trust me."

Harris gave a sharp snap. Jester froze. Its head tilted. A beat passed. Then—*splat*. A sticky glob of pink saliva hit Harris squarely in the eye. Adam started laughing. Harris cursed, wiping at his face, unamused. The Court Jester chirped proudly and fanned its frill.

TWENTY-FOUR

THE WIND PRESSED STEADILY against Adam's jacket as he walked eastward on the plateau. The ship lay far behind him, like a forgotten relic. Before him, the landscape rolled outward in waves of brittle sediment—sun-bleached, pitted, and soft underfoot. Cracks covered the crusty surface, revealing flaky layers beneath. Sedimentary rock, he guessed. Probably some extraterrestrial analog to shale or siltstone. It broke easily when he prodded it with his boot, and he could peel the layers apart with his fingers. It felt unstable. Like a skin stretched over the skeleton of something older. Something more solid.

Soon, Adam reached the outcropping. It jutted from the rusty plateau like a ship's prow—dark, defiant, and distinctly different from the stone around it. He was so distracted before that he hardly paid attention to its composition. Up close, the difference was striking. Gone were the soft edges of weathered sediment. Here, the rock was hard, fine-grained, and unyielding to the tapping of his climber's hammer. He ran his palm along it—cool and smooth. It glittered faintly where fractures caught the light. A metamorphic stone, maybe. Possibly igneous, though it lacked the bubbling texture of basalt or pumice. It reminded him of something much closer to home.

Devil's Lake.

The memory hit with force: towering bluffs of purple quartzite rising from a Wisconsin prairie of sandstone and glacial till. Quartzite is formed when sandstone undergoes intense trial by the application of heat and pressure. As with the human soul, it is not destroyed. Rather, it is transformed by time and tectonics into something nearly indestructible. The quartzite cliffs that ringed the mile-long lake had once been sea-bottom sand, but now stood above the waves like time incarnate.

Adam grew up in the shadow of Devil's Doorway—a bridge-like opening in the quartzite cliffs formed by the serendipitous placement of several stones weighing thousands of pounds each. Adam's great-grandfather owned a cabin on the north shore of Devil's Lake during the great depression. His father took Adam to the lake often when he was a child. In the fall and summer, he'd free climb the cliffs, ignorant of the risks he was taking. In the winter, he explored the bluffs on cross-country skis. At the age of fourteen, Adam met a mountaineer who taught him how to climb using a harness, ropes, and anchors. That led to his first lesson in lead climbing. The following year, he traveled west to try his hand at climbing big walls. Then a friend invited him on a trip to Denali. He was hooked.

Adam entered the passageway, his hand tracing the cleaved faces and jagged seams. "Same story," he whispered, "different world."

Beyond the opening, he caught glimpses of more tunnels and grottos twisting further into the plateau. The organic shapes were like the innards of a great beast. There was a raw, simple beauty to the place that stirred something deep within him—a longing for freedom, unbound by the artificial structures of men.

Adam moved between the rock walls, half-expecting a shape to emerge from their tangle at any moment.

Nothing did.

He crouched and waited, feeling the passage of time, until, at last, he gave up hope of finding anything there. He left the deserted grotto behind and walked a few hundred yards further, squinting into the red sun's light.

He looked north toward the mountain range and saw something new. The lower peaks to the west appeared as he had always seen them. But on the tallest spire, a red cloud had formed that obscured the entire upper half of the mountain. The sky was otherwise cloudless. Some local phenomenon caused the mass of dust on the mountain.

Adam walked eastward following the terrain downhill until a familiar sound caught his attention. He tilted his head to listen.

Water.

He felt a flicker of hope. It was some distance away, but it was unmistakable. He followed the sound and, in a few minutes, arrived at the bank of a shallow stream that carved its way through beds of silt, the water barely covering the polished stones beneath. Thick mats of moss-like plants covered its banks, branching out into myriad forms of plant life. Strange ferns with jointed stems filled one bank, and starburst clusters of fungal blooms filled the other.

The creek flowed south, quickening its pace as it meandered toward an unseen destination. The dying sun cut stark shadows across the planet's surface as it raced toward the horizon. Adam knew the alien world would soon turn dark.

He stepped across the shoal, each stride cautious and deliberate. After landing on the other side, he scrambled up a ridge. At the top of the rise, he saw a larger valley further to the east. The massive pink planet that Harris called Madreon sat high in the night sky, providing better illumination than a full moon on Earth.

Adam continued eastward, the terrain sloping ever downward as he walked deeper into the broad valley. Again, he heard the unmistakable sound of running water. He found a straight draw that made for easy hiking and followed it. The sound of water grew louder as he approached a riverbank.

And there they were.

At least a dozen of them—tall, columnar beings, each rising from the riverbank like stone pillars. Their matte surfaces spiraled upward with faint ridges. Each one glowed softly from within, emitting a cool blue-green light that pulsed gently across their surfaces.

Adam stepped closer and felt a faint downward pull as if the planet's gravity had increased. The nearer he came to the river, the more gravity pulled him downward. He stepped cautiously toward the nearest Zenolith, his footsteps muffled by the thick, mossy ground cover. At the bank's edge, he sat down, dipped his hand into the river, and cupped a small amount of the liquid in his palm. It wasn't water. The fluid exhibited a viscosity similar to that of mineral oil.

The Zenolith did not react to him. He observed a nearby specimen. Its base seemed to be fused to the ground, though he was sure it could move. There were no limbs in the usual sense, but he could see slender tendrils extending from its base into the shallows of the river as if drawing something up from the current. Adam pulled an empty bottle from his pack and filled it from the river. He replaced the cap, then stowed it away.

Finally, he spoke. "Hello." The word echoed with unexpected force across the tranquil valley. The beings held their positions, unmoving. Not a stir. Not a flicker.

He closed his eyes and waited for the Zenolith to send a visual message. He sensed nothing. He already knew he could communicate with them even if they did not respond in the moment.

Then, he sensed it—the feeling as if something or someone was watching and evaluating his every move.

Or his every thought.

He arose, noting again the increased pull of gravity. He didn't want to leave, but it was already dark. He turned back in the direction from which he had come and began the long trek back to the ship.

When he was out of sight of the river, Adam noticed that the gravitational anomaly had disappeared.

After entering his report into the computer, Adam sat in the chair in the dayroom, his elbows resting on the edge of the desk. The water bottle, filled with liquid from the river, sat upright on the desk, capped and glistening under the overhead lights.

"You covered a lot of ground," Major Harris said. "Did you stay within the three-mile radius?"

"As far as I can tell. I took compass bearings. The terrain was mostly plateau and open draw. There's a stream to the east of the outcropping and a larger river beyond it."

Harris looked at him. "You went beyond the outcropping?"

"I figured it was worth a look. I wasn't planning on going that far, but the Zenolith weren't where I previously saw them. The terrain was navigable, and I heard running water. That's where I found them gathered near the riverbank."

"How many?"

"Twelve, maybe fifteen. All stationary." He pointed at the bottle. "They seemed to be drawing that liquid from the river through tendrils located in their base."

"Any signs of communication?"

Adam shook his head. "I spoke to them but they didn't respond. I spent a few minutes checking for visual messages, but there weren't any. Just stillness. Like I wasn't even there."

Harris made a few notes on his tablet. "Describe the river."

"It's wide and shallow. The water—or whatever it is—has a viscosity similar to mineral oil. Strange surface tension. The river flows south. The banks were thick with plant life. Ferns, moss, fungi. An entire ecosystem crammed into a sliver of valley."

"I see you collected a sample." Harris picked up the bottle, turned it slowly in his hand, then unscrewed the cap. He retrieved a shallow, metallic dish from a specimen kit in a desk drawer and poured a small amount of the liquid into it. Under the white overhead light, the sample revealed its actual color—a shimmering pink. Harris crouched closer, narrowing his eyes. He donned a glove from his pocket, dipped a finger in, and rubbed it between his fingertips. "Reminds me of something," he said. "Years ago, a friend of mine was injured in a blast —IED in a tight alley in Kabul. Shrapnel caught him in the chest, but the real damage was the concussion. Closed head injury. Swelling. They had to drill."

Adam waited for Harris to finish his anecdote.

"They placed a bolt in his skull to monitor his intercranial pressure. There was a drainage line—clear tubing, feeding into a little bag that hung on the side of the hospital bed. It collected cerebrospinal fluid." He tapped the edge of the dish. "It looked just like this."

Adam smiled. "Most people have no appreciation for how the skilled use of a drill and a well-placed bolt can save your life."

Harris gave a knowing smile. "Radiation monitor?"

Adam unclipped the monitor from his jacket and slid it across the table. Harris pocketed it with a nod.

As Adam zipped his empty pack, he paused with the zipper halfway closed. "There are two more things I should tell you."

Harris looked up. "Go on."

"There was a strange feeling when I was at the river."

"What feeling?"

"The feeling that I was being watched. Not just watched, but judged. And not by the Zenolith. Something else. Like… maybe the river itself is conscious."

"Do you think the river is… alive?"

"Maybe."

"What's the second thing?"

"It's about the river. As I walked closer to it, the force of gravity increased. I felt a definite downward pull, the closer I got."

"Are you sure it was the river and not the Zenolith?"

"I've met the Zenolith a couple of times, but never felt a change in gravity. A change in energy maybe, but this was different. I think it's coming from the river." He looked at the dish. "Maybe we should ask Jester."

Harris didn't respond. His eyes narrowed, and suddenly, he stood. "Thanks for the report." Without waiting for acknowledgment, he turned and exited through the far door, leaving Adam alone with the pink liquid.

TWENTY-FIVE

ADAM CROUCHED BESIDE A LARGE BOULDER, the dawn light washing the plateau in a soft, violet hue. In his gloved hands, a small creature wriggled—its frill fluttering faintly, flickering in quiet rhythm. Court Jester tilted his head, as if sensing what was about to happen.

"You've been good company," Adam said. "A little weird... but a good friend."

The wind carried the sounds of insects. Somewhere out there, others like Jester moved freely—flickering in and out of sight, vanishing with a shimmer.

Adam exhaled slowly. "I can't keep you," he said. "I know what it's like to be a captive. I could never do that to you."

He opened his hands.

Jester didn't flee at first. The creature remained still in Adam's hands, its antennae twitching, its limbs poised as though waiting for a signal. Then, with a shimmer of motion and a ripple of shifting color, it leaped from his palms and darted across the ground toward the rocks, a blur of motion and light.

Adam watched it disappear beneath a fibrous plant that bent slightly, as if bowing in acknowledgment.

He smiled. "Freedom suits you."

The echo of his own words stayed with him. They weren't just for Jester. They were for himself.

He turned and made his way back toward the ship—lighter somehow, though he carried nothing at all.

TWENTY-SIX

THE DOOR to the dayroom slid open, and Adam stepped through, blinking as he took in the unmistakable change. The room's far wall—a seamless panel of brushed steel—was now set several feet farther back. In the expanded space stood a device unlike anything he had ever seen. It rose from the floor, smooth and dark, with a module on the near side that housed a small light fixture. Cables trailed from its base, disappearing into the floor.

Major Harris stood beside the machine, his arms behind his back, watching Adam. "Your birthday present arrived, but they forgot to wrap it."

Adam chuckled while studying the machine. "What does it do?"

"It's a bumper car. We thought you needed a little entertainment."

"Huh. Nice present."

Harris took a seat at the desk. Adam sat opposite him.

Harris picked up his tablet and began scrolling until he came to a page displaying a sequence of acronyms.

SIGINT. HUMINT. IMINT. MASINT. OSINT.

He handed the tablet to Adam. "These are intelligence disciplines," Harris said. "Signals, Human, Imagery, Measurement and Signature, Open Source. There are others—more obscure ones—but these five are the bedrock of what an intelligence officer does. We collect signs. Indicators. Echoes of things that are or were. We analyze them. We extrapolate patterns. We try to understand the story behind the noise."

"What does this have to do with me?"

"You read the terrain," Harris began. "You evaluate snowpack. Determine the speed and direction of ocean currents. Note cloud formations and make weather assessments. You evaluate the qualities of rock. You see the story behind them. What came before, and what's likely ahead. The most skilled outdoorsmen in the world read signs like scripture. That's what you do."

"When you live outdoors, you have to know what's around you."

"True," Harris said. "But I've seen your file and I read the Carlton case. A murder with no witnesses, no weapon, no leads whatsoever. And you saw it before it happened."

Adam looked away.

"I'm not trying to spook you," Harris continued. "I just want to acknowledge something most people would rather ignore. There's another intelligence discipline. One that doesn't fit into the neat categories on my screen. It's something else entirely."

Adam looked at Harris. "You're saying this is why I'm here."

"I chose you for a reason."

"What reason, exactly?"

Harris motioned toward the machine. "The device behind me doesn't officially exist. Even within the program, only a few people are aware of it. It's a new prototype based on a larger and older model. It's designed to interface with the mind, not through language, but imagery. It was originally built for intelligence officers who experienced high-stress, high-fidelity premonitions."

"Premonitions..." Adam repeated.

Harris smiled. "Visions, if you prefer. The machine creates... or displays visual projections. The projections allow the user to observe possible future events. The scenes aren't guaranteed outcomes—they're fragments from one of many possible timelines."

"Possibilities?" Adam clarified.

"Exactly," Harris said. "The early tests, although promising, produced unpredictable results. Some of the information gathered was useful. Much of it was garbage. The machine's developers learned that some people are more adept than others at seeing and interpreting the data. They didn't expect to find someone whose entire neurological profile was already tuned for it."

"I'm not a radio."

"You see things, my friend. You track meaning. You catch signals that others miss."

"So, you brought me on this mission because I'm a walking anomaly."

"I brought you on this mission because I believe that anomaly is the entire point." Harris's expression darkened. "You never took a formal psych eval, but I didn't need one. I'd been building a profile on you for months from the digital breadcrumbs you left behind."

Adam shifted uneasily in his chair. "Like what?"

"You quit your job at Ridgeline, broke up with Lisa, didn't renew your lease, and vanished with no forwarding address. You tried to kill yourself, then stopped answering messages from anyone who knew you. Hell, I didn't think you'd answer me when I sent you that text posing as a recruiter. And somewhere in there, you started drinking again—just enough to numb the pain."

Adam's gaze shifted to the floor.

"To the analysts, you looked like a slow motion trainwreck. PTSD flags, depressive markers, avoidance behaviors. They said you wouldn't climb if I ordered you. You'd crack under pressure."

"They weren't wrong."

They may have been right, but that's not the whole story. To me, it meant you were already untethered. No strings, no job, no partner, no place to call home. If you disappeared for a year, no one would ask questions. That made you a liability on paper, but it also made you the perfect asset for a clandestine program. I caught hell for picking you. But I knew that if I could get you to climb—if you chose to—that what you'd find up there wouldn't be just another pile of biologic data. It would be insight. Revelation, maybe."

"Sounds like you went to bat for me."

"I did," Harris replied. "Speaking of revelation... I need to ask—how does it work? This gift of yours. What exactly do you see?"

"There are layers to it," Adam said. "Sometimes, I'm shown things that are completely literal—down to the last detail. In those moments, it's like I've been pulled to a place or a time. I'm not imagining it. I'm *there*. What I see is exactly what's happening—or what *will* happen. There's no interpretation needed. I just observe and make note of it."

"Is that what you saw with the Carlton murder?"

"Yes."

Harris glanced down at his tablet and jotted a quick note. "And when it's not literal?"

"Then it's symbolic. Impressions, images, phrases, metaphors. It comes from the same source, but the message is coded. I have to interpret it. And that's where things get tricky."

"How accurate are those symbolic ones?"

"It varies. Sometimes eighty percent. Sometimes fifty... and sometimes zero. I've misread things before. Especially when I was younger. It's not the message that's flawed—it's the receiver."

"So, it's a question of skill?"

"And humility. I've learned not to assume too much. Symbolic images can be powerful, but they don't always mean what I want them to mean. Confirmation bias can take an interpretation in the wrong direction. The biggest risk is thinking I've got the meaning all figured out when I don't. I try to leave my interpretations open—to allow for alternative explanations."

Harris typed a note into the tablet. "That's helpful." He tapped his stylus against the edge of the tablet, then looked up. "I think the risk is worth it. We're walking into a situation with no precedent. Standard intelligence disciplines aren't going to cut it. Even if what you give us is partially symbolic and partially literal—it's more than we'd have otherwise."

"So, you want me to try that machine?"

"If you're willing. Your profile suggests you're particularly suited to interface with it. We believe your mind may naturally sync with the projection field, making the visions clearer—and perhaps more accurate—than what others might see."

Adam looked at the machine with uncertainty. "What exactly do you expect me to find?"

"I don't know. But anything you see could prove useful."

"Alright. I'll try it."

He rose from his chair, approached the machine, and sat down, leaning back into the seat. Harris toggled a switch, and the device responded. A low rumble emanated from within, like the roll of distant thunder. The air grew warmer. The rumble evolved into a high-pitched hum that resonated in Adam's chest and behind his eyes.

Then, holographic images shimmered into view—dim at first, then brightening into clarity. Adam saw himself stumbling through a vast desert. The cracked earth baked beneath a blood-red sun that hung low and heavy in the sky. Heat waves twisted the horizon into a mirage. He moved with desperation, his skin blistered, his eyes hollow. Columns of sand rose around him like ghosts, shifting and relentless.

The image faded.

Next, he was climbing a mountain. The air was thin. He gasped and struggled to breathe. He was dizzy and disoriented. Then, he collapsed.

The scene dissolved.

The next image was silent and still. He lay submerged at the bottom of a body of water, unmoving. Scarlet light filtered through the water's surface, distorted and shimmering. Sediment curled in gentle eddies around his body, which rested as if asleep—or dead.

Adam looked at Harris and motioned for him to shut the machine off. Harris flipped a switch on the remote control, and the machine began to wind down. The hum dropped in pitch, then fell away completely. Adam sat still for a moment, breathing slowly.

Harris stepped forward. "What did you see?"

Adam described the three scenes. "They felt real. Not like dreams. Like... I was there."

"Possible, but unlikely," Harris replied.

"Do these things actually happen?"

"To our knowledge, what you saw are events from a possible timeline. Not guaranteed.

Adam stared at the now-dark machine, a chill creeping into his limbs despite the warmth it had given off. He stepped away from the machine and took a seat at the desk. Suddenly, the accident on the Ingraham Glacier filled his thoughts. Tears welled up in his eyes.

Harris noticed the change. "What is it?"

"They were good people. Mark and Jennifer. They trusted me."

"They followed your lead," Harris said, "because you were the best."

Adam shook his head. "It doesn't matter. I led them into a death zone. I ignored the signs."

"You couldn't have known what would happen."

"*I had a vision*," Adam said sharply.

Harris stared at him.

"Just before the ice broke. I saw it in my mind. I saw Jennifer. I saw the ice collapse. I was given a warning and I ignored it."

"Jesus," Harris said softly. "Did you tell anyone?"

"Who would believe me?"

"Would *you* have believed you?" Harris let the question hang unanswered. "Look, even if you *had* told them—they would've thought you were joking. Or rattled. They would've smiled, maybe laughed. And then they would've continued."

"You don't know that."

"Not with certainty but I can guess. Because I know people. And you do too. Same reason you wouldn't have signed up for this mission if I'd told you the truth from the start."

"It's not the same."

"It's *exactly* the same," Harris exclaimed. "You can give someone all the right words, but if they're not ready to hear them, they won't." Suddenly, Harris sat back, his face brightening. "You know... we might be able to find out."

Adam gave him a puzzled look.

"The machine," Harris said.

"What about it?"

"I've heard that it doesn't just show the future. It can show the past. And I think that under the right conditions, it can be directed. The observer can shape what's seen, maybe even choose what they want to explore."

"You're saying... I could sit for another session and ask the machine to show me what would've happened if I warned them."

"That's exactly what I'm saying."

"And if I see that they ignore me..."

"Then maybe it's time you stop punishing yourself for something you couldn't prevent."

"But what if they *do* heed my warning and turn back?"

"Rock and a hard place, my friend. It's your call."

Adam considered the possibilities. He wasn't sure what was worse—believing they may have ignored him and continued, or knowing they would have turned around and headed home, alive. He looked at the machine, then at the door to the outside world. He got up and sat in the center of the viewing platform. "Turn it on."

Harris got up, walked toward the machine, and powered it on. It cycled through its startup routine.

Adam closed his eyes and thought of the tragedy on Mount Rainier. The scene resolved around him. He was on the Ingraham Glacier again. Mark and Jennifer were just ahead of him, silhouetted against a distant ridge. They turned, laughing about something. Mark held his ice axe. Jennifer adjusted her pack. Adam stood there, watching them, and spoke aloud in his mind:

"What would have happened if I warned them?" he asked. The scene shifted. Adam saw himself stop mid-step, calling out to them.

"I saw something!" he shouted. "A warning. We need to turn back."

Jennifer tilted her head, confused. Mark frowned. "You look a little pale. Is the altitude getting to you?"

"No," Adam said firmly. "I'm serious. Something's coming. A collapse. I saw it."

Jennifer glanced at Mark, then smiled. "Adam, we're fine. We're *finally* out here, I don't want to go back. Even if something happens, you've trained us on what to do. Come on, let's get to the summit."

He tried again. "Jennifer, I'm telling you we have to turn back—*now!*"

This time, they paused longer. Mark scratched the back of his neck, not sure who he should listen to. "Hey, Jen, he seems pretty certain. Maybe we should go back."

Jennifer sighed, "Guys, nothing bad is going to happen. If we turn around now, I'll regret it forever. Let's just get through this section before the weather changes, and then we can reassess things."

They turned and continued up the ridge. Moments later, the sound came. The thunder-crack of shifting ice. A scream. Then silence. The vision dissolved.

Adam signaled for Harris to kill the power to the machine, then sat there quietly.

"Well?" Harris asked.

Adam looked at Harris, "I warned them but they didn't listen."

TWENTY-SEVEN

ADAM STEPPED out onto the plateau in the early light of day. The ship's skin shimmered softly behind him and disappeared as the hatch sealed shut. Adam took a deep breath, then began moving east. The shallow canyon faded behind him, dissolving into the morning haze. His path to the rock outcropping had become instinctive. He traced the rise and fall of the land, stepping over patches of waxy ground cover and clusters of vegetation. Alien plants flexed and pulsed as he passed, drawing energy from the low-angle sunlight. Further from the ship, the faint chirr of unseen insects echoed off the rock walls—a syncopated beat that joined his march.

When he had reached the outcropping, he tilted his head back and studied a tall boulder that towered above the others—an oblong spire of stone rising nearly seventy feet high. Its jagged face was streaked with bands of minerals. Its top was wide enough to offer a view of the valley. He traced an imaginary line in his head and figured he could reach the top without using aid.

"You've done this a million times," he said to himself. His palms were wet with sweat. He rubbed them in the dirt, then took a breath and exhaled slowly. He eyed the route one more time, dropped his pack, and tested a few handholds. Satisfied, he began the ascent. His fingers and boots found purchase in the rough crevices as he moved upward. The rock was cool beneath his hands, not yet absorbing heat from the early morning sun. Halfway up, he wedged his hand in a crack and made a fist, then relaxed his body while pausing to catch his breath. He scanned the stone above, looking for a route around a shallow overhang. He withdrew his hand and moved up the route once again. After a careful sidestep, he continued upward and finally pulled himself onto the top of the spire with a grunt.

From this vantage, the terrain opened wide before him. The valley to the east, with the stream he had encountered on his last trip, carved a dark path through the rocks southward. However, farther to the north, he spotted an alternate route: a ridge that traced a direct line toward the larger river valley beyond. It cut through the landscape, bypassing the winding course of the smaller stream entirely.

That's the path, he thought.

Adam lingered only long enough to log the line mentally. He pulled out the camera Harris had given him and snapped a photo, then made his way carefully back down the rock face. Small stones scattered beneath him as he fell the final few feet to the plateau.

After shouldering his pack, he began the new route. The ascent of the ridge was steady, but the terrain was easier than he had expected. Sparse vegetation clung to the rise, some spiny and coiled, like fossilized vines, others wide-leaved and trembling in the breeze. As he crested the ridge, the valley came into full view—a sweeping basin of layered rock and dense alien flora buzzing with life. He descended into it, each step drawing him closer to the distant shimmer of the magenta water. The sound of the river finally reached him, and he followed the slope to its edge.

And then, he felt the sensation again—the feeling as if a pair of eyes were observing him.

He continued toward his destination. As he neared the river, he felt an increase in the downward pull of gravity—the same one he had experienced before. It intensified as he drew near the riverbank.

At last, the river lay before him, wide and slow, its surface rippling in the vermilion glow of the morning sun. Alien life clustered at its edge —twisted plants, translucent twigs, and the titanic Zenolith standing still on the bank of the river. He snapped more pictures.

Adam stepped off the stone ridge and onto a soft, flat patch of ground near the river's edge. His boots sank slightly into the spongy soil, and he had to steady himself. It felt as if someone had slipped a lead jacket on him, and that feeling triggered a thought.

What if the pull of gravity itself is a message? Who is sending the message?

He took off his pack, lay down on the ground, and closed his eyes. Instantly, a voice boomed in his mind.

"How can we help you, Walker?"

Adam's eyes flew open, but he remained still. *Who said that?*

The voice had not come from the Zenolith, he thought. It seemed to come from the river itself.

He slowed his breathing. Then, the voice returned. "We mean you no harm." The words washed over him like warm water.

Adam's tension eased. In his thoughts, he replied: *Thank you. I mean you no harm, either.* The moment the words had formed, a vision filled his mind. Red liquid tumbled over smooth rocks, curling down the plateau. The current picked up speed, rushing over a ledge and cascading down a rocky precipice. Thousands of feet below, the water formed a river that cut through a vast desert. Then, the voice spoke again—firmer this time.

"You must go there."

Adam lay on the ground, pondering the message. While unexpected, the meaning was clear. He had been directed to explore the region below the plateau.

But why? He thought.

He waited, but there was no answer. He rose from the ground, shouldered his pack, and began the hike back to the ship. As he walked, the river receded behind him, but its presence lingered—like a weight pressed gently against his back. It was comforting, but he couldn't place why. Perhaps it made him feel less alone. Adam climbed the ridge in silence, the downward pull now gone, replaced by a curious sense of propulsion.

He retraced his steps along the ridge's spine and then moved toward the outcropping. He reached the familiar canyon and followed the path to the ship, pausing at the threshold, glancing over his shoulder toward the distant river. The words still echoed in his mind.

You must go there.

Adam sat at the metal desk in the dayroom. The pack lay unopened on the floor beside him. Major Harris stood across the room with the stoicism of a soldier, hands behind his back, his face devoid of expression.

"I reached the river valley shortly after first light. I took a new route that bypassed the stream and the canyon floor. There's a ridge trail that leads straight there."

Harris nodded. "And the Zenolith?"

"Same as before. At least a dozen of them. Stationary. Unresponsive. But I didn't go there for them this time. I went for the river."

Harris's gaze sharpened. "Why the river?"

"The last time I was near it, I had a strange feeling. I wanted to see if it would happen again, so I could more confidently attribute it to the river as opposed to something else."

"Fair enough. And did you experience it?"

"I did, and then some. I laid down beside the water and closed my eyes. Within seconds, I heard a voice. Not an audible one. It was in my mind."

Harris smiled. "A hallucination?"

"No," Adam said firmly, then added more carefully, "At least, I don't believe so."

"What did it say?"

"It asked, 'How can we help you, Walker?' Then it said, 'We mean you no harm.'" Adam removed the camera from his pack. "I responded telepathically. I said I meant no harm either."

Harris listened.

"I saw a vision. Water—pink, like the river—cascading down rocks, across the plateau, and then over a cliff, into a desert below. Then the voice returned and said, 'You must go there.'"

Harris moved to the side of the desk and leaned against it. His eyes searched Adam's face. "And you're sure this wasn't a dream, a projection, something your own mind generated?"

Adam didn't answer. He stared at the desktop.

Harris continued. "Intelligence analysts grade information on a scale from low confidence to high, based on the likelihood that a report is factual. Is there an objective way to verify that you were, in fact, speaking with a sentient being, and not just experiencing an internal conversation?"

Adam looked up, annoyed. "Let me ask you something, Major. Ever operate a radio on a crowded frequency?"

"Plenty of times."

"So, you know what it's like. You're on a ship. Or a plane. Fogged in. You can't see another vessel. But you hear it—a signal—cutting through the static, through the chatter of other ships, other aircraft, and background noise. The signal is still there. It's not a hallucination—not something you imagined. It's a message sent through a medium. And you received it—because your receiver and your ears were tuned for it."

"I thought you said you weren't a radio."

Adam chuckled. "You picked me because you supposedly trust my 'tuning.' If you want to take advantage of that, you're gonna have to trust that I know the difference between my own thoughts and someone else's."

Harris pursed his lips. "I guess you have a point. Please, continue."

"The voice didn't belong to me. It didn't sound like me. It didn't feel like me. It was external—but it was made audible by a part of my mind that knows how to listen."

"At the very least," Harris said, "you believe you were contacted by something intelligent. Something real."

"I do."

"That last message—'You must go there.' What's your read on that?"

"Obviously, they want me to go there. Whoever 'they' might be. By 'there' I assume they mean the desert below the plateau—it's important. I don't know why, but I'm meant to go there."

"That changes the mission profile."

"Does that mean you're going to break protocol? Please tell me we're going to break protocol."

Harris stood still, unamused.

Adam rose from his chair, took a few steps toward the bedroom, then stopped. "If I had my gear, I could do it."

Harris walked toward the exit. *He wants to go. That's a good sign,* he thought. He turned back. "We'll discuss a new plan in the morning. Get some rest. You may need it."

TWENTY-EIGHT

THE NEXT MORNING, Adam and Major Harris sat at the desk in the dayroom. "I want you to consider another viewing session with the machine," Harris said.

"What, you want to see all the *other* ways I could die out there?"

"It's my duty to inform you that you're not allowed to die without my permission."

"I'll keep that in mind," Adam replied. "Other than scaring the hell out of me, is there a reason why you want me to do another viewing session?"

"I think it might show more of what's coming. We've already confirmed that it can be guided. You just need to use your will and steer it in a direction. The first time, it likely picked up on your fears, as those were the strongest subconscious elements."

Adam studied Harris for a moment, then sighed. "Alright."

Adam rose, approached the machine, and then sat, leaning back into the seat. Harris activated the machine. Adam felt a low vibration beneath him. Lights flickered, then steadied. The low rumble built into a high-pitched hum.

Adam spoke his request: "Show me what I need to know about the future." Suddenly, a scene appeared before him. A long, polished table stretched across a dark room, illuminated only by pinpoints of soft light that glowed above each seated figure. There were no windows. No walls were visible—just the table and those around it. Men and women —dressed in suits, uniforms, and robes—sat in silence as one man stood at the head of the table.

"Our position is now uncontested," the speaker said. "The populations of Earth are fragmented, distracted. All that remains is consolidation."

Another figure leaned forward. "What about the other planets?"

"We're confident that we can bring them into the alliance... including Opturius."

An elderly man in a robe spoke: "Our high priest has foreseen trouble on Opturius. He's not convinced it can be... civilized."

"That's what they said about Madreon," the first speaker replied, "but look at it now. We have a team exploring Opturius. Let's wait for their findings before writing it off as a loss."

A middle-aged man in a uniform spoke: "Opturius may be difficult. But if we cannot integrate its inhabitants, they will be neutralized. They will not stand in the way."

A murmur of agreement rippled through the room. The vision faded. Adam signaled to Harris to shut the machine down. He stood up, stepped away from the machine, and walked toward the desk in stunned silence. He took a seat.

Harris stood just a few feet away, watching him. "What did you see?"

Adam looked at him. He waited, swallowed, then began. "Some sort of meeting. Maybe a council. Approximately fifteen people. They seemed powerful. They were calm. Cold. They talked about Earth like it was already conquered. Like its people didn't matter anymore."

"What kind of people were they? Military? Government officials?"

"Some looked like politicians. Some were in uniform. Others wore suits. One wore a robe. Different accents, different backgrounds, different allegiances—on the surface. But they were united. And they were planning."

"Planning what?"

"To consolidate control. To use Earth as a kind of hub. A command center maybe. And to expand outward. To other worlds."

"Did they mention Opturius by name?"

Adam nodded. "Yes. They said Opturius may be difficult. If they can't integrate the inhabitants, they'll be neutralized."

Harris's face remained unchanged. "Then we have work to do."

Adam looked up at him curiously. "This doesn't seem to surprise you."

"The purpose for this mission is classified. Congratulations Mister Walker, you just received a classified briefing."

"There's one more thing," Adam said nervously. "A man said they have someone exploring Opturius. Was he talking about us?"

"No. I told you we were sent here to mitigate a crisis. Those people either have sent or will soon send a team here. Our team was thrown together quickly and sent here to learn about Opturius in the hope of preventing them from fulfilling their plan."

Harris motioned for Adam to follow and led him into the adjacent room—the one Adam had dubbed the "bedroom." Against the wall stood the row of lockers. Harris approached them and then spoke clearly. "Open locker number three." With a soft mechanical click, the third locker from the left swung open. "Open locker number four."

Another door opened, then a third, then a fourth, until all the lockers but the three furthest to the right stood open.

Adam stepped forward to examine the contents. Each locker was meticulously organized with his mountaineering gear: his climbing harness, carabiners, ascenders, crampons, stoves, gloves, belay devices, ropes, insulated clothing—all packed in logical groupings, neater than he had ever stored them.

"You kidnapped my gear too? How did you find it?"

"We have ways."

Adam looked at his equipment. "Why are you showing me this?"

"I want you to scout the approaches to the tallest mountain to the north. I'm not asking you to climb it. I just need is to know if it's climbable."

Adam glanced at the gear and then at Harris. "I'll give it a shot."

Harris smiled. "Good."

"Speaking of shots… you got any booze on this rig? There's nothing to *do* here except mission related crap. How do you stay sane?"

"This isn't a party ship. You're thinking of the navy."

Adam threw up his arms in disgust. "Well, next time I'll ask the navy to kidnap me."

Adam looked at a spool of rope in the ninth locker. "That's not mine."

"We brought extra static line," Harris said, his voice tinged with amusement. "Can't have you whining about not being adequately prepared."

Three lockers remained unopened. Adam pointed to one of them. "What's in those?"

"Equipment that will only be needed under certain circumstances,"

Harris said. "You haven't yet committed to the mountain, so for now, you don't need to worry about what's in those lockers."

TWENTY-NINE

THE SUN HAD JUST CLEARED the eastern rim of the canyon when Adam stepped onto the plateau. Behind him, the ship sat silent, half-submerged in a sheen of dust. Before him, the land sloped gently upward—rolling rises of red rocks and brittle foliage reaching toward the ragged silhouette of the mountains.

Major Harris's request had been simple: Scout the approaches to the tallest peak. See if it can be climbed. There had been no pressure. No deadline. Just a suggestion that he walk the area around the base of the mountain and identify potential difficulties and access points. But it was enough to stir something in Adam's gut—a quiet fire that mixed anticipation with old fears.

The terrain to the north was easy enough: wind-etched rock, scattered boulders, dry streambeds cutting shallow channels through the plateau. As the morning wore on, the mountains that seemed small on the horizon now towered, rugged and imposing. The tallest peak stood apart from the others, its shoulders steep and proud, crowned by a halo of wind-sculpted cloud. Even from this distance, Adam could see that the summit cliffs were sheer, formidable in a way that wasn't obvious from the ship.

He stopped just shy of a shallow ridge and unclipped his field scope from his belt. Through the lens, the details emerged: stratified layers near the base, likely softer sedimentary rock. Higher up, the tone changed. There was harder stone. Cleaner fractures. He studied the visible lines of ascent—ridges, buttresses, snowless couloirs etched by erosion. No obvious path presented itself.

He spent the day exploring the terrain east and west of the peak's base before returning to the southern slope, jotting notes as he went:

> *East and west approaches are steep and rugged. The south side has a gentler rise.*

Regardless of the approach one might take, the difficulty, Adam surmised, would be the summit.

> *Summit: Sheer vertical faces near the top. Aid required. Route finding will be a challenge.*

He added a note at the bottom of the page:

> *No snowfields. No ice. Sandstone lower down? Quartzite or granite up high?*

There was no commitment yet to climb. It was just a recon mission.

The airlock hissed open. Adam stepped inside, brushing windborne grit from his collar.

Harris sat at the desk. "You're back," he said, without looking up.

Adam slid into the opposite chair and set his field notebook on the table between them. "I scouted the south, east, and west flanks. I've got some initial impressions."

Harris gestured toward the notebook. "Let's hear it."

Adam opened to the most recent page and turned it toward Harris. "The tallest peak is climbable—well, maybe. It won't be easy. The lower portion of the mountain looks like soft sedimentary rock. The kind of stuff that flakes when you look at it wrong."

"Sandstone?" Harris asked.

"Something like it. But as you move higher, the color and composition shifts. Harder strata. That's good. There would be reliable anchors near the top."

"What about the approaches?"

"The east and west sides are steep, ugly, and there are no coffee shops. The south side seems like the best bet." Adam stared for a moment at the wall behind Harris. "There appears to be a summit plateau, maybe a quarter of a mile wide."

"You said it's climbable. If you were going to climb it—hypothetically, of course—what would it take?"

Adam smirked. "Hypothetically?"

"Spitballing."

"There's no snow or ice to contend with, which helps—but it would take a lot of equipment and planning. The atmosphere is unknown. It might require oxygen depending on the weather and whether the hypothetical climber is prone to altitude sickness. It would require hauling gear up vertical faces and establishing at least two base camps. Maybe three. The first base camp is obvious—at the foot of the mountain. Looks to be about five miles from the ship. The second would be higher, maybe four or five thousand feet up. The third—if needed—would be somewhere near the cliffs below the summit."

"What would be an estimated timeframe to get to the summit and back?"

Adam hesitated. "Best case, four to five days. That's if everything goes well—weather, health, terrain. But it isn't a known route. It's not even a known mountain range. There's no satellite data, no weather models, no idea if there's meltwater or springs."

"Food and oxygen caches?"

"Gear would need to be hauled in stages. Oxygen would be stashed at the second base camp, maybe a spare tank higher. Food would be dehydrated. Jetboil stoves, fuel canisters, water filtration gear... assuming there's a source of water. Otherwise, all water would have to be packed. And so far, I've only seen that pink stuff."

"What about the overall risk?"

"Unknown. All of it. A climber could be socked in by wind for three days. Or make it halfway up and hit a sheer wall that no human could ever ascend. We're not on Earth, Major."

"Your observational skills are excellent, Walker."

"They landed me this luxurious job, didn't they?"

Harris's eyes drifted from the notebook to Adam. "You nervous?"

"Of course. But not the way I was. And for the record, I'm still not committing to climbing."

"Didn't ask you to."

THIRTY

ADAM STEPPED beyond the ship's main hatch. His chat with Harris left him with mixed feelings. The wind had calmed. Just a breeze brushing the canyon walls.

He hadn't planned to walk far— just stretch his legs and breathe something besides recycled air. His muscles ached from stillness. His thoughts were looping, chasing themselves like dogs around a track. He needed to get out.

With his boots crunching softly on the stone, Adam followed the perimeter ridge that cradled their vessel. The stars here burned with a clarity he hadn't seen since his last winter in Alaska. *No light pollution here,* he mused.

He paused at a rise in the terrain, just high enough to see the full silhouette of the mountain range to the north. The tallest peak stood above the others like a sentinel.

Something caught his eye. A light on the summit. It wasn't bright. Just a glow of light where there shouldn't have been any—pale and cool, with a bluish tinge, as though the mountain had exhaled something luminous.

Adam squinted. The light wasn't blinking. There was no flicker and no obvious source.

What the hell?

He stepped forward. Then, as quickly as it had appeared, the light vanished. Snuffed out like a candle. He stayed there for a minute, waiting, but it didn't return. He turned and walked back to the ship.

Harris was at the desk in the dayroom, reviewing notes on a tablet. He looked up as Adam entered.

"You look like a man with something on his mind," Harris said.

Adam unzipped his jacket and dropped into the chair across from him. "I got a little stir-crazy, so I took a walk."

Harris nodded. "I know the feeling."

"I saw a glow."

"A glow?"

"It was on the summit of the tallest peak. A pale blue light like someone turned on a lantern. There was no movement. No defined shape. Just light."

"You sure it wasn't a reflection? Maybe an aurora?"

"I don't think so. It didn't reflect. And if it was an aurora, it would still be there. It was there for a few seconds, then it was gone."

"I'll make a note," Harris said. "We'll keep an eye on it."

THIRTY-ONE

ADAM LAY ON HIS BUNK, one knee propped against the wall, the other foot resting flat as he stared at the notebook. He pressed a mechanical pencil against his lips, his eyes narrowed in thought.

It's just for fun. He had told himself that three times now. He'd sketched the massif from memory—its broad flanks, the banded layers of soft and hard stone, and the summit rim that dared someone to ascend it. He flipped back two pages to a topographic sketch, then forward again to a list of possible staging points:

> Base camp 1 - plateau, Base camp 2 - ledge, 4-5K ft, potential Base camp 3 - sub-summit shelf?

Below it, he'd scribbled:

> Water access?
> Anchor-friendly zones
> Exposure risk (wind tunnels?)
> Haul line feasibility

He made a list of gear that would be required.

> *Jetboil + 2 fuel canisters*
> *Bivy sack + thermal liner*
> *O2 tank x2 + regulator (staged Base camp 2, backup Base camp 3)*
> *Static + dynamic lines, cams, chocks, draws, pitons (soft rock backup)*
> *Protein powder, dehydrated meals, chocolate*
> *Weather station*

He paused. "Not like I'm actually doing this," he said aloud.

The bunk was silent in reply. He stared at the hand-drawn route lines again. His mind replayed the terrain.

He flipped to a blank page and titled it:

> *Contingency Plan – Emergency Descent*

He stopped and stared at the words. That was the moment he knew. He was planning how to survive a bad turn of events. Which meant he'd already decided to go.

He heard a knock on the door. "Come in."

The door slid open, revealing Kyle Casey standing in the corridor. The medical officer stepped inside and let the door close behind him. "Are you busy?" he asked.

"Just making notes in case I decided to take Harris up on his request."

"Are you thinking of climbing the mountain?"

"I'm considering it."

"The last time we talked, you were looking for an excuse to disappear.

Panic attacks, tremors, dissociation, and the thousand-yard stare I've seen a hundred times in evac tents."

"I remember."

"But here you are. Not just surviving, but planning to tackle the mountain." He paused, watching Adam's face. "How'd that happen?"

Adam glanced down at his hands, then back up. "I got some air. Faced a few demons. You were right about forgiving myself. Ever since then, I've felt better. Like there's a purpose for being here."

Casey studied him, then pulled out his tablet and tapped a few notes. "You've been eating regularly?"

"Yeah."

"Nightmares?"

"Some. Less intense. They're manageable."

"Any suicidal ideation in the last seven days?"

Adam's eyes didn't flinch. "No."

Casey nodded. "Any visual anomalies? Auditory hallucinations?"

Adam hesitated. "I saw something on the summit. Some kind of light. But I don't think it was my mind playing tricks."

Casey gave a half-smile. "You're not the first mountaineer to talk about mysterious lights. But that's not my call to interpret." He set the tablet down. "You're definitely more stable."

"Still a mess though?"

Casey chuckled. "I don't know anyone who isn't. You're just one with an upward trajectory."

"So I'm cleared?"

"With conditions." Casey's tone sharpened. "Any further trauma—physical or emotional—and I want to see you immediately. No slipping under the radar. No stoic mountaineer bullshit. You crash again, and I'll pull the plug. Understood?"

"Crystal clear."

"One more thing," Casey said, "Don't put too much pressure on yourself. Whether you climb or not, every crew member on this ship is on your side." He turned and left the room.

THIRTY-TWO

THE LURE of climbing the as-of-yet unnamed mountain had been too much for Adam to resist. After all, he had been handed an opportunity to ascend a peak no other alpinist would ever see, much less set foot on. Internally, the decision had already been made. Now, the external preparation began.

Climbing gear covered the desk in the dayroom. Coils of rope. A chalk bag. Carabiners. Portable stoves. A sleeping bag rested on top of the computer terminal. On the chair's seat was a sling that held an array of chocks, cams, hexes, and nuts—mechanical devices inserted into rock formations to serve as anchor points for ropes. Adam sorted through everything, mentally checking off boxes.

He had been content to use the small day pack provided by Major Harris to explore the plateau. It was light, and it served its purpose. But a trip to the summit of the mountain would require more gear than a day pack could hold. Harris had brought Adam's expedition pack in case it was needed.

Major Harris watched him intently.

Adam looked up. "Normally, I'd have a team for this. At least two others—three's ideal. Shared gear, someone to help manage ropes, belays, hazards. Soloing a peak like this isn't exactly best practice."

"You're not getting a team," Harris said.

Adam sighed. "Figured you'd say that. In that case, I'll need to make several trips up and down the route to cache gear—staging equipment at locations between here and the summit. Before I start hauling oxygen tanks, I'd like to get a clearer picture of the air density and pressure up there."

"You want to conduct weather tests."

Adam nodded. "If I can get some basic readings—barometric pressure, wind speed, oxygen level—I'll know whether I'm going to black out halfway up or not."

"I can provide a portable weather station. Small, packable. How long would you need?"

"One or two hikes. A few hours to log the data. If the readings come back within range, I'll plan the summit push after that."

"I'll get you the weather kit."

"I'll start sorting gear caches tonight. First trip will be tomorrow."

Harris frowned. "Remember who's in charge here."

Adam raised an eyebrow. "Do *you* want to climb this mountain?"

THIRTY-THREE

THE FOLLOWING morning in the dayroom, Adam paced, testing the weight and balance of the expedition pack. The weather station was secured inside next to a rolled bivy sack, ropes, packages of freeze-dried food, water, and a small stove.

Thianos hung low in the sky, casting long red streaks across the plateau as he stepped away from the ship and hiked north. The mountain's silhouette draped the horizon. The landscape felt quiet—watchful, even—but there were no signs of Zenolith. The hike was long and uneventful.

When he reached the base of the mountain, Adam found a flat section of terrain among a scatter of boulders, partially sheltered by a sloping rock face. It would become base camp one. He unloaded the equipment he would not need for the short trip up the mountain to gather weather readings.

Next, Adam studied the route on the southern approach that seemed most promising. He stood there for several minutes, sipping water while analyzing the path and committing it to memory, then adjusted his pack and began the climb.

The ascent wasn't technical, but it demanded focus. Adam moved slowly, avoiding loose gravel and taking advantage of natural steps where erosion had exposed flat, hard surfaces. The route took him up several thousand feet along a series of slanted rock slabs and compacted soil shelves. The sun climbed with him, casting shifting shadows behind every ridge and boulder. The air was dry and thinner but still breathable. By mid-afternoon, he had reached a broad ledge near a break in the ridge—high enough to provide the needed weather data and safe enough to rest.

Adam lowered his pack to the ground and sat with his back to a sun-warmed boulder. He unpacked the weather station and assembled it. He drove a small anchor stake into the soil and mounted the sensor, then flipped a switch. A soft chime indicated the station was active.

Wind speed. Barometric pressure. Oxygen concentration. Temperature gradients. All data points began scrolling across the screen. Adam watched for a while, then retrieved a protein bar from his pocket and chewed it as the station collected its readings. He recorded observations in his notebook, marking fluctuations over several hours. The oxygen levels were lower than he'd hoped for, but not dangerously so—at least not at this altitude.

Satisfied, he powered down the unit, packed it away, and began his descent. The climb down was less strenuous, but he was still cautious. The light was shifting fast now.

By the time Adam reached the plateau again, the sky had deepened to burgundy. Stars were beginning to show. Upon reaching base camp one, he unrolled his bivy sack, set up his small stove, and heated a mug of water, adding a package of freeze-dried lasagna to it. As he ate, he glanced up at the stars emerging above the mountain. He knew most of the constellations in the night sky on Earth, but none of the stars visible now were like the ones back home.

Home.

What is home to me now?

Though the food he ate was warm, he shivered. A longing came over him that he couldn't quite pinpoint. He searched these strange new stars as if they could quell that longing. The world around him was still and silent, save for the occasional whisper of wind swirling through the rock. Adam lay back, his hands behind his head, the sky opening above him like a door. In a few days, he'd go higher. But tonight, he would rest.

THIRTY-FOUR

THE AIR WAS STILL and cool when Adam awakened. He packed quickly but left most of his gear—ropes, stove, spare food, and the weather station—tucked into a shallow alcove at base camp one. He covered it with a tarp weighted down with stones before turning back toward the plateau.

The return hike to the ship was quiet. Adam moved steadily across the alien landscape, his breath forming small puffs in the chill air. By mid-morning, he reached the canyon where the ship lay cloaked. He advanced, his hand outstretched until it met the smooth, unseen surface. The hatch opened silently, and he stepped inside. Major Harris was already waiting in the dayroom.

Adam dropped his pack and took a seat at the desk. "I made it to the base and climbed a few thousand feet, set up the weather station, took readings, and made camp overnight before heading back."

Harris took a seat. "Show me the readings."

Adam pulled out the notebook and showed it to Harris. "Barometric pressure was lower than expected. Oxygen levels were thin. Winds were 10 to 20 knots. No sign of storms or pressure swings."

Harris reviewed the numbers, his eyes scanning quickly. "Any sign of intelligent life?"

"Not yet. But I didn't go high enough for a full survey. That's next."

"Speaking of life..." Harris pulled out a pen and scribbled in Adam's notebook the preassigned names of the next two intelligent beings: *Tharnak* and *Aerum*. "Just in case," he said. "So, what's your plan?"

"I want to return to base camp one. From there, I'll climb higher, another four to five thousand feet, and find a location for a second base camp—somewhere to cache additional gear and supplies. Once that's in place, I can plan a summit attempt."

Harris nodded. "You're confident in the plan?"

"Nothing's guaranteed, but I think it's doable."

Harris stood. "Then it's approved. Take what you need."

Adam tore a sheet of paper from the notebook—a pencil drawing of the mountain. He removed a roll of tape from the desk drawer, tore off a piece, then affixed the drawing on the wall above the desk.

He spent the next hour gathering gear—additional water, food, and climbing hardware. He packed with precision, double-checking every item and calculating weight and redundancy. The fear he initially harbored about the climb seemed far away. Perhaps, it was only hiding.

THIRTY-FIVE

THE NEXT DAY, Adam was back on the plateau, heading north toward the shadow of the great mountain. Base camp one came into view just after midday. The wind had picked up, filling the air with dust, causing him to breathe harder. The cache of gear he'd left the day before remained untouched. He approached it slowly, scanning the horizon out of habit, but nothing moved. He drank water as he ate a handful of jerky, but he didn't rest long. He needed to find a suitable location higher on the mountain to stash more equipment and obtain more weather data.

Route-finding in unexplored terrain is a matter of eliminating poor choices rather than following an obvious path. Adam's eyes scanned the ground ten to fifteen feet ahead. His mind in real time rejected bad footing choices and loose rocks, while directing his feet to the places less likely to cause him to stumble. Still, loose gravel scattered occasionally under his feet, the uneven ground forcing him to find his balance with every step.

He moved steadily, trying to keep an even pace and conserve energy. The terrain changed with elevation. The soil gave way to smooth, slanted slabs of soft stone, heat radiating skyward from their sun-soaked surfaces. Small bursts of wind kicked grit into the air. Thianos cast a sheen like spilled wine across the ridges.

Adam paused at the next bend in the trail, breathing deeply. The air was getting thinner, making him winded more easily. After resting, he continued moving upward.

As he walked, a ledge opened behind him, offering a view back toward the plateau and the land beyond it. He turned and stood there for a moment, sipping water. At the southern horizon, an ocean—or perhaps a large lake—melted into sky. Adam had no idea that a large body of water was nearby. *I'll bet Harris didn't bring my kayak*, he thought. To the west, the broken lines of the canyon gave way to basins and long ridges. To the east was the valley of the great river. To the north was the summit. Still distant. Still waiting.

He drank slowly, letting the wind pass over him. Then he pressed on. Another three thousand vertical feet brought him to a narrow shelf tucked beneath a wind-scoured cliff.

The ledge wasn't perfect, but it was the best option available. It was mostly flat—weathered but stable. There were no erosion cuts. No signs of falling debris. Just enough space to stake down a bivy and stow gear away from the edge.

He had found base camp two.

Adam exhaled as he slipped off his pack. His shoulders screamed with relief. He knelt, stretched out the stiffness in his legs, and began unloading equipment. Food. Water. Blankets. Fuel. He stacked the gear neatly against a wall and covered it with a tarp held down by stones.

The wind here had more teeth. It whipped around the cliff face and moaned through the cracks like a forgotten hymn. Adam found a spot exposed to the wind, assembled the weather station, and powered it on. The screen flickered to life, casting a pale green glow. Numbers scrolled slowly across the display. He scribbled in his notebook the temperature and the drop in oxygen. Barometric pressure was low. The wind speed was 30 knots with gusts to 40 knots.

The environment wasn't exactly hostile, but it wasn't friendly either. When Adam had obtained the data he needed, he packed up the weather station and began the descent.

By the time he had returned to base camp one, Thianos was descending behind the ridgelines. The open sky drew heat from the stone, chilling the air. Adam set up camp and settled in for the night, the sky above him deepening into lavender.

Stars blinked into view one by one. He lay back against the packed gear, watching the light fade. Tomorrow, he would return to the ship.

THIRTY-SIX

THE MORNING AIR was crisp when Adam stirred. Stars scattered across the sky like softening sparks, reluctant to succumb to the sunrise. He lay still for a few minutes longer, watching the slow shift of color from burgundy to dusty pink.

Adam hadn't dreamed. Or perhaps he had, and the mountain had kept the memory. Either way, he felt different. A clear sense of purpose had etched itself in his mind.

He broke camp and hoisted his pack into position. The hike back to the ship wasn't difficult, but he felt mild pain in his knees, a slight ache in his back, and burning in his calves from the climb the day before. He also felt a growing sense of confidence—that of a man who had walked with revelation long enough to trust it. His thoughts became a list of factors working both for and against him.

Harris said there is opposition to the mission.

The people I saw in the meeting want to enslave or destroy life on Opturius.

The Zenolith knew my deepest thoughts and offered counsel.

The river gave me instruction.

Are the forces of Opturius working with me?

If so, are they powerful enough to help me complete the mission?

What exactly is the mission?

Adam paused before the canyon and glanced back. The mountain waited, rising majestically above the rusty plain. Somewhere far below, a river flowed. Somewhere beyond that, the sea waited, silent and watching.

The ship's airlock sealed shut behind Adam. He stood still near the entrance, allowing his eyes to adjust to the artificial light. The air was sterile after days of breathing dust. He exhaled slowly, then dropped his pack just inside the door. It hit the floor with a thud. He peeled off his gloves. They were stiff with sweat. The scent of his own body clung to him—soil, exertion, and time.

In the dayroom, Major Harris sat at the desk, a tablet balanced across one knee. He sniffed once and wrinkled his nose. "You need a shower."

Adam smiled. "Nice to see you too."

"I'm ready for your report," Harris said.

Adam sat in the chair opposite Harris. "I established base camp two—I'd say five thousand feet higher. There's a ledge, maybe three feet wide. Just enough room to pitch a bivy and store gear. I set up the weather station and let the sensors cycle for two hours." Adam pulled out his notebook and handed it to Harris.

Harris glanced at the readings and frowned. "Pressure's low."

"Can confirm. Oxygen is… suboptimal."

"You'll need supplemental oxygen."

"For the summit push, definitely. I'll need to cache the oxygen—at or above base camp two—then acclimatize before a summit attempt."

Harris handed back the notebook. "We need to troubleshoot some obvious problems."

"What do you have in mind?"

"That summit is ten, maybe twelve thousand feet above this plateau."

Adam rubbed his chin. "That's—what, Everest from Tibet?"

Harris continued, "The atmospheric pressure here is lower. If this data is accurate, Opturius has about 70% of Earth's sea-level pressure—give or take. Oxygen content is similar, maybe slightly richer, but it's the partial pressure of oxygen that matters."

Adam followed his thoughts. "Lower total pressure means lower oxygen pressure. So even at modest elevation—"

"—You'll be operating at the equivalent of 24,000 feet on Earth," Harris concluded. "And you've got no acclimatization. No red blood cell ramp-up. And no time to get it."

"What about Diamox?"

"Best case, it gives you a head start. But it's no substitute for red blood cell mass. And it's not fast enough in this window." Harris shook his head. "To raise hematocrit meaningfully, you'd need a month or more in a hypoxia tent—or time at progressively higher base camps."

"What about oxygen? High-flow. I've done it before."

Harris stared at him in silence.

"That's not going to work either, is it?"

"Oxygen helps, sure. But here, you're dealing with a thinner atmospheric column overall. Even with high-flow, your margin is razor-thin. And if you get pinned down in a storm for three days, you won't be able to carry enough tanks to ride it out. Adaptation beats tech."

"So what are you saying—that I shouldn't try?"

"I'm saying we planned for this." Harris rose from his chair and walked toward the bedroom. Adam followed. Major Harris was not a mountaineer on par with Adam, but he was familiar with the sport. He'd hiked the Olympics once a month as a ritual. When the assignment to Opturius came his way, he used his time to learn all he could. The two men passed through the doorway to the bedroom.

Major Harris stood before the three unopened lockers and spoke. "Open locker number ten."

The locker swung open. Harris retrieved a metal case, opened it, and handed Adam a slim silver canister. "Ever hear of Xenon?"

"Isn't it used in anesthesia?"

"Yes, but there are other uses. It turns out, when it's inhaled, Xenon stimulates erythropoietin release. It fast-tracks red blood cell production, eliminating the time needed for acclimatization."

Adam grinned. "You think it'll work here?"

"I think it's your best shot. And I wouldn't offer it if I didn't believe it was safe. Well... safe-ish."

Adam turned the canister over in his hand. "So instead of three weeks at base camp, I inhale this and what—become altitude-proof?"

"Not exactly. You'll still need to acclimatize, but it'll take a fraction of the time. It should delay hypoxia, and maybe prevent pulmonary edema. But you'll need this, too."

Harris reached into the locker and pulled out what looked like a matte black thermos and handed it to Adam.

"What is it? Compressed regret?"

"A GasTec Microtank. It's pressurized to twenty thousand psi. Equivalent to a rack full of oxygen tanks."

"You're kidding."

"Military grade composite material. Stronger than titanium, lighter than aluminum. And it won't explode if you drop it."

"What's the catch?"

Harris gave a half-smile. "Don't breathe too fast."

Adam ran his thumb over the regulator's dial. "If this thing works as you claim, I might actually make the summit."

"It works," Harris said. "Just don't try to refill it without a station rated for twenty thousand psi. This isn't something you top off with a bicycle pump."

Adam set the tank on the bed and pointed to the next unopened locker. "What's in there?"

"Open locker number eleven." The locker opened. It held two plastic cases. Harris pulled the first case from the locker, set it on the bed, and popped it open. Nestled inside was a sleek, dark device slightly larger than a man's fist.

"This," Harris said, "is the Ascension Unit, Model VX-3."

"Ascension unit?"

"Since you won't have anyone to belay you, you'll need help. This little baby feeds you rope as you're climbing and manages rope slack. The onboard sensors monitor your body movement and it locks when it senses a fall."

Adam whistled. "A fancy GriGri."

"A GriGri that doesn't get distracted texting its ex when you're dangling by three fingers on an overhang."

Adam rolled his eyes. "That would never happen."

"You clip it to your chest loop, thread the rope, and it becomes your personal guardian angel."

Adam gave a small, impressed nod. "Alright. What's in the other case?"

Harris removed the case from the locker and handed the case to Adam, who opened it, removed a device, and set the case on his bed. He examined the device, turning it over in his hands. "It looks like a Z2R."

"Close," Harris said. "The MLU is a mechanical leverage unit. Nicknamed the MULE, it's a modified version of the Z2R haul device. The good people at DARPA upgraded it with a safety system. Unlike the original, this one has an active module that provides automatic locking in the event of a load shift, tension loss, or fall. The system detects descent speed, line angle, and acceleration using onboard sensors and deploys a locking pin inside the gear track.

Adam opened the device and fed a length of rope through it.

Harris continued. "It can handle static and dynamic ropes from eight to eleven millimeters. It has an auto-adjustment mechanism that calibrates rope compression and friction angle. You're looking at about five million taxpayer dollars in a device that climbs for you and babysits the haul bag at the same time."

"And they let you walk off with one of these?"

"We're in an exclusive club. Membership has benefits."

Adam studied both devices with dawning respect. "So, the VX-3 gets me up the route, and the MLU brings the gear behind me?"

"Exactly. The VX-3 is your lifeline. The MLU is your sherpa."

Adam set the device on the bed. "Can I ask what's in the last locker?"

"You may or may not like this one," Harris said. The locker opened at his command, and he pulled out a black case. He set the case on the bed, opened it, and stood back.

"Geez," Adam said. "Is that what I think it is?"

"Ladies and gentlemen, allow me to introduce our next contestant." Harris picked up a small drill. "This is the Talon 9. It's compatible with the MULE and provides the needed horsepower for hauling heavy loads up cliffs. Its sensors allow it to adjust torque in real-time based on load weight and rope tension. If the power is cut or the drill fails in the middle of a lift, the clutch engages automatically and arrests the load. No manual intervention is needed."

Harris set the drill down, lifted a black cylinder from the case, and handed it to Adam. "This is for when the stone starts spitting out your cams."

Adam turned the cylinder in his hand, then twisted open the top and dumped out an assortment of drill bits and mountaineering bolts.

"Diamond-tipped bits," Harris said. "The bolts are titanium. They don't need epoxy in most materials. But if you need it," he added, picking up a tube from the kit, "this epoxy sets in ten minutes."

"Thanks, boss, but I don't use bolts. I prefer to climb clean."

"I know. And I respect that. But it's not like Opturius will be added to the national parks list any time soon. If you don't need them, fine. But if you do, they're at your disposal."

THIRTY-SEVEN

MEDICAL OFFICER KYLE CASEY pushed a cart into Adam's bunkroom. On it was the Xenon tank, a mask and supply line for administering the gas, a cardiac monitor, and a medical bag.

Adam glanced up from his bed, where he'd been organizing climbing cams and chocks like sacred relics. "Is this the part where you shoot me full of radioactive isotopes and wish me good luck?"

Casey chuckled. "Worse. It's time for your Xenon treatment. Full disclosure—I've never done this before. I had to read up on Xenon. It's a volatile noble gas known to cause mild dissociative effects. It should reduce neural overactivity and dampen any residual anxiety you're having. It might prevent you from flinging yourself off a cliff."

Adam patted the mattress beside him. "Ah. A romantic gaslight evening. All we're missing is a violinist and a bottle of wine."

Casey ignored the comment and opened a pouch of electrodes. "I'll need you to lie down." Adam reclined on the bed. Casey attached electrodes to Adam's skin and connected EKG leads, then obtained a set of vital signs. He removed the Xenon canister from its case, then connected a mask to it, and slipped it over Adam's face.

"I always imagined my first time would be in a spa. With candles."

Casey opened a valve on the tank. A hiss whispered from the regulator. "Ten minutes, light dose. Breathe normally. No sudden revelations or prophetic insight unless previously authorized."

Adam smirked beneath the mask. "Will I finally understand the meaning of life?"

"That's statistically unlikely."

At first, Adam felt nothing. Then, a song drifted through his mind, followed by blackness.

"Welcome back," Casey murmured, watching the EKG screen.

Adam stirred. His eyes fluttered as he sang off-key: "Fly me to the moon, let me play among the stars... let me see what spring is like on... Jupiter and Mars."

Casey laughed as he slipped the mask off Adam's face. He removed the electrodes and stowed the gear on the cart.

As he prepared to leave, Adam leaned back on his elbows. "Hey, Doc?"

"Yeah?"

"If I die on this mountain, there's some high-quality chocolate in my locker."

"I'll make sure it gets into the right hands."

THIRTY-EIGHT

ADAM RETURNED to base camp two the following morning. In his pack, he carried the equipment Major Harris had given him, along with other supplies. Once there, he unloaded the gear. Upon arriving, he was dizzy, nauseous, and short of breath—symptoms of altitude sickness. He administered oxygen to ease the symptoms, then got to work setting up base camp.

The ledge formally known as base camp two was narrow—no more than three feet wide—and angled just enough to make Adam nervous. One misplaced step and the drop would be fatal. With all its drawbacks, it was the best location available. Above him, the sloping terrain steepened into cliffs; below, the world dropped away into shifting rock and dust.

The rock here was soft and offered poor anchoring by the usual methods. After giving the matter considerable thought, Adam had decided Major Harris was right. Leaving no sign that you'd been on a mountain is an excellent ethic for heavily traveled routes, but no one would know if he drilled a few holes and set a couple of bolts to secure his gear on the ledge.

He drilled two holes in the stone six feet apart, brushed the debris from the holes, blew out the residue, and for safety, squeezed a glob of epoxy into each hole. Next, he assembled the hangers and tapped the bolts into place with his climbing hammer. Ten minutes later, the epoxy was set. Adam clipped a carabiner and sling to a bolt and gave it a hard tug. There was no sign of movement. He tested the other bolt, which seemed just as solid. Now, to set up camp.

First came the bivy sack. It wasn't a tent—there was no room for that. The bivy is a streamlined, weather-resistant cocoon barely larger than a sleeping bag, with a breathable outer shell. He found the flattest portion of the ledge, cleared away loose gravel, and unrolled the sack. The bivy sack had small anchor loops sewn into the corners. Adam clipped them to the bolts. The zippers were stiff from dust, but they closed tightly. Inside, the bag was insulated with a thin mylar lining—enough to retain body heat without causing sweat to condense. Adam unrolled his sleeping bag and placed it in the bivy then crawled inside to test the fit. It was tight. Barely room to roll onto his side. But it would do.

Next, Adam crawled out of the bivy and scouted higher ground, climbing a few hundred feet to test his lungs. It wasn't an easy climb. He needed supplemental oxygen, but he slowly made his way upward along a series of rock shelves. Then, he heard the sound of water. Two hundred yards west, he found a small stream that cascaded down the mountain. He pulled two bottles from his pack and filled them, then retraced his route. Back at base camp two, Adam prepared to treat the so-called water he had collected from the stream. He flipped his headlamp on and inspected the liquid. It was the same pink, viscous fluid he had found at the river. He ran it through a filter. There was no change in color or viscosity. His mind rehearsed the warnings he had heard from others—ones he had parroted himself over the years—about drinking from an unknown source.

"Whatever doesn't kill you, makes you stronger," he said, "I guess I'm having pink lemonade."

Adam reached into his pack and pulled out his stove: a metal cylinder no wider than his wrist. Its fuel canister was half-spent. He screwed the pieces together, sparked the piezo igniter, and smiled as a blue flame leapt to life. He boiled some of the pink liquid. His meal tonight was rehydrated curry lentils with rice. He dumped the contents of the pouch into the hot pink liquid, gave it a stir, and a few minutes later, it was ready to eat.

He leaned back, cradling the hot food against his chest. The lentils were salty, textured with bits of chickpea and freeze-dried tomato. Not gourmet, but high in carbohydrates, and that's what mattered.

After the meal, Adam cleaned his cookware with a few splashes of water and a scrap of cloth. He flung the wastewater over the edge then stowed the equipment.

He inspected his harness, anchor points, and rope. There were no frays. No slippage. He checked his vitals. His heart rate was 110. His oxygen saturation was 85 percent. Not ideal, but not life-threatening. He settled into his bivy and journaled.

Day one at BC2: Climbed higher. Found a stream with the same liquid as the river. Filtered and boiled it, but it didn't change. Pulse 110. Oxygen low. Headache and nausea. No signs of life besides insects.

Adam slept through the night and awakened at dawn. He crawled from his bivy, and, with an empty pack, save for water and dried food, he returned to base camp one, loaded the gear he had stashed there, and made for base camp two. He arrived at the higher camp still dizzy and nauseous. Until he had acclimated, it would be foolish to move toward the summit. He decided to remain at base camp two until the symptoms resolved.

In the evening, he prepared a meal. When he had eaten, he cleaned his utensils, then settled in for the night journaled.

Day two at BC2: All gear moved to BC2. Pulse 100. Oxygen 84. Short of breath. Mild headache and nausea. Remaining at BC2.

As night fell, the wind picked up. The bivy sack rustled like a whispering shroud. Adam drew the zipper up to his chin, tugged his beanie low over his ears, and closed his eyes.

As daylight faded, the wind intensified. Dust howled across the rock slopes, and small stones pelted the bivy like shrapnel. He tightened the drawstring and pressed himself flat against the wall behind him, trying to make himself one with the rock.

The wind didn't relent. Hour after hour, it raged, tumbling pebbles into his sack. Waves of sand piled up against him, creeping over his chest, his legs, and his face. The sound was deafening.

Adam couldn't sleep and was barely able to breathe. He lost track of time. His mind spun with thoughts he couldn't stop.

Would the bolts fail?

Would the ledge shear away?

Would the entire slope collapse?

The air inside the bivy grew thick with dust. Adam adjusted the vent flap, but only drew more grit inside. He passed into a semi-lucid state —not quite awake, not fully asleep.

And then—silence.

As quickly as it had come, the wind was gone.

Adam stirred but had difficulty moving beneath the weight of sand and debris. He rolled onto his stomach and made a passageway for his nose and mouth, then slowly lifted himself from the ground, allowing the sand to roll off the bivy. He wriggled his way partly out of the sleeping bag then turned and opened the bivy's zipper. His gloved fingers pushed up through packed debris. A gasp escaped him as the bivy tore open and his head emerged, coated in dust and coughing from the grit in his throat.

The ledge was buried. Adam sat up slowly, wiped his face, and spat dust from his mouth. He rose and surveyed the damage. The ledge, though covered in debris, was intact. He unclipped the bivy, extracted the sleeping bag and rolled both of them up, then brushed away the sand and stones. Though the wind had tried to erase him, the summit still waited. And he intended to reach it.

THIRTY-NINE

AFTER CLEARING AWAY the debris from the windstorm, Adam considered his next move. He was still dizzy and nauseous and became short of breath with mild exertion. Succumbing to the high-altitude edition of Groundhog's Day, he opted to remain at base camp two, where he spent the day resting. The goal was to give his body a chance to acclimatize. In the evening, he ate, and journaled, then fell asleep.

He awoke in the morning and, for the first time since arriving at base camp two, he did not have a headache and was not nauseous. *Finally,* he thought, *time to move higher.*

The stone above base camp two was suboptimal. Flaky is nice when you're making biscuits, but flaky rock won't hold a chock or a cam when loaded. He spent the better part of the morning scouting lines on the south-facing wall above base camp two, hoping to find a clean route that avoided the crumbling fractures and weathered pockets. But everything here seemed sketchy—especially under load.

He tested a cam in a shallow crack. He gave it a tug. It held. Then he weighted it.

Snap.

The lobes of the cam popped like a champagne cork, sending it flying past his helmet.

Next came the placement of a nut in a tapered opening in the rock. It was a classic constriction—textbook, at least in theory. But the rock wouldn't bite. He pulled on it and it dislodged with a puff of dust.

He knelt on the exposed stone and stared up at a diagonal seam just overhead—a line that swept right across the face toward a narrow ledge maybe fifty feet up. *That's the way,* he thought. *If I can just get off the ground safely.*

But the crack was too shallow for cams, and nuts would not hold. It required something else. He sighed and reached into his pack and pulled out the case containing the drill and bolts.

He remembered the first time he had climbed *The Nose* in Yosemite—an ascent that made his fingers bleed and his ethics ache. Even back then, he'd wrestled with the question: *When does exploration justify the scars it leaves behind?*

Some scars are worth it, he thought. *And let's face it, Opturius isn't exactly a tourist destination.*

Besides, he told himself, *if I can't get up this wall, the mission stalls.*

The ascent would require a bombproof anchor at the bottom. Normally, a solid tree or massive boulder would do, but there was none. Using his hammer, Adam tapped the rock at the base of the route and located a solid section. He pulled the drill from its case, made a hole, cleaned it, filled it with epoxy, and set the bolt. He set a second bolt a few feet away. Ten minutes later, he tested them. They passed with flying colors.

He secured a sling between the two bolts to equalize the load and anchored one end of his climbing rope to the sling. Next, he threaded the running end of the rope through the VX-3 that was clipped to his chest loop. The device would self-feed rope as he climbed, and lock instantly if he fell. Climbing rope stretches under weight, so a climber is not injured from deceleration during a fall.

As one climbs, one would usually set cams, chocks, or nuts at intervals, clipping a quickdraw—a length of nylon webbing with a carabiner at each end—to each piece of protection, allowing the rope to move freely. A fall leaves the climber suspended from the last piece of protection they set. Since the rock on this route was soft, Adam opted to set bolts instead of the usual protection.

He laced up his rock climbing shoes, double checked his gear, chalked his hands, and eased onto the face.

The first few moves up the wall were smears—a technique where the sole of the shoe presses against an irregularity in the rock, providing a foothold. After several moves upward, Adam braced himself with three points of contact and pulled the drill from its holster. He pressed the bit against the stone and drilled. Dust clouded the air. The bit sank quickly. He switched off the drill, brushed the hole clean, grabbed a bolt, pressed it in, then twisted the head until it clicked and expanded.

He took a deep breath, leaned into it, and then bounced once.

It held.

Solid as granite. He laughed out loud. "Well, I'll be damned. Guess you're for real."

The second bolt went in faster. The hole was clean. No epoxy was needed. He clipped the rope to it and glanced down at the route behind him. Suddenly, the whole thing seemed possible.

Adam worked his way higher and eventually reached a ledge, where he set another bolt, and secured a pulley and a second rope. He descended the route, packed a haul bag with equipment, and clipped it to a separate static line. At the base, he activated the MULE. The motorized system, powered by the drill, hauled the load with efficiency. He then ascended the route a second time, removing gear as he went.

Adam moved steadily upward, ascending cracks and contoured rock faces, each time, hauling his gear behind him. At last, he reached a broad ledge where he could rest. He snacked and rehydrated before continuing.

Above him, there was another wall. The most promising line followed a long, clean crack that spidered up the face like a lightning bolt frozen in stone. He set an anchor, checked his gear, chalked his hands, and began.

The first section flowed like music. The crack was wide enough to be friendly, and narrow enough to offer protection. He ascended by jamming his hands and feet alternately in the crack and placing cams as he moved higher.

But the crack ended, and he came to a dead stop. Above him stretched ten vertical feet of blank rock—featureless save for a faint bulge halfway through. No knobs, and no pockets.

He took a deep breath and began his next move. He felt confident. The second move required a long reach. The third was a smear and press. On the fourth move, his hand slipped and he dropped. The rope went taut, tugging on the anchors. His body swung gently in place, suspended like a pendulum.

"Not this way," he muttered.

He re-entered the crack and ascended until he came to the crux and traversed right this time, onto a narrow band of ledges.

Not as elegant, but it might work.

The holds were small but usable. The first few moves went well. Then the line curved slightly, and the wall pushed him out. He reached and slipped.

The rope caught him, but not before he swung wide and smashed his right side into a pointed rock spur jutting from the face.

Pain erupted in his ribs. He hung there, groaning, unable to speak, barely able to move. Blood soaked his shirt, oozing through the fabric near his side. He pressed a couple of fingers against his ribs and felt the movement of bones. Then slowly, gingerly, he downclimbed. Every step was agony. The movement sent jabs through his traumatized torso like a sharpened spear.

Hours later, back at base camp two, he stripped off his shirt and cleaned the wound, a long gash across his ribs that was bruised and swollen. He wondered if he had sustained rib fractures. And for the first time, he was concerned that Opturius may have bacteria that could cause a fatal infection. He smeared antibiotic ointment on the gash as a precaution, then wrapped it tightly.

The delays were beginning to add up. Adam knew Harris would worry about him, so he pulled the radio from his pack, turned it on, and keyed the mic. "Harris, this is Adam with a status report." There was no reply. He tried again, "Major Harris, this is Adam, do you copy?" Still nothing.

"It figures." Adam set the radio down and opened the flap of the pack. A gust of wind kicked up, sending the radio tumbling over the edge before he could stow it in the pack.

"Shit... just what I need." Adam shook his head, let out a sigh, and crawled into his bivy. The summit felt a thousand miles away. He was cold, tired, hungry, and sore, and it was almost dark. As he lay beneath the stars, he considered his options.

Maybe this is the end.

There's no shame in stopping.

You've done more than anyone else ever has.

You can walk away.

But another voice whispered louder.

You didn't come here to walk away.

The injury might slow him, but it would not stop him. He would rest. And then he would climb again. At least there was no wind tonight.

Adam awoke just before dawn with pain stabbing at his ribs. It would be foolish to attempt the route again in his present condition, so he opted to rest for the day. As evening came, he checked his gear and journaled.

Night draped the mountain in silence. Adam lay curled inside his bivy sack, his breathing shallow, his body cocooned against the cold rock. Pain radiated from his side, dulled by exhaustion. He had eaten little. Sleep had come fitfully at first, but when it came, it pulled him deep.

He didn't stir when the light arrived. It was soft—a pale shimmer against the dark stone, like starlight caught and magnified through mist. It settled on the rock face, then moved across the ledge where Adam lay.

There was no sound. Just the delicate glow of light. Inside the bivy sack, Adam twitched but did not wake. His breathing deepened. And the dream took shape.

He was back on the cliff wall—not as a climber, but as an observer. The route glowed with clarity. A crack revealed itself where he'd seen only shadow. Foot placements suggested themselves. A left-hand reach curved unexpectedly upward to a hidden hold. The entire route became clear.

When morning broke, the light was gone. Adam woke and noticed his ribs were no longer sore. He sat up slowly, rubbing his eyes. Then he paused. As he recalled the dream, a certainty about the route settled in his mind.

He packed his gear, then turned to face the cliff again. He used the anchor and protection he had set the previous day. With each move up the route, his confidence grew. Every feature matched the scenes he'd seen in the dream. Even the tiny quartz inclusion near the traverse—a marker he hadn't noticed before—gleamed in the morning light, just as it had glimmered in the night.

Finally, he reached a ledge just wide enough to accommodate his equipment. He set a bolt, clipped in, and breathed a sigh of relief. Above him, the final wall awaited, hard and clean. It would not be easy, but he knew it could be done.

Adam deployed a pulley and a second line and descended, then set up the haul system and brought his gear to the higher ledge that would become base camp three.

Above him, the crown of the mountain awaited—120 feet of steep, vertical defiance. There would be no detours now. No alternate routes. The summit was directly overhead. He would reach it or die trying. Between oxygen treatments, Adam set up camp on the narrow ledge, where he spent the night, plotting his assault on the summit.

In the morning, he awoke dizzy and nauseous, but the symptoms cleared with a single treatment of oxygen. He made a quick breakfast, then turned his attention to the summit.

Adam scrambled higher, but the air was thin, and he found himself panting and needing oxygen more frequently. He scanned the cliff above him. Unlike the sedimentary layers below, this section of rock was dark and dense. No flaking, no crumbling. He tapped it with his hammer and smiled at the sharp feedback.

Solid rock. Finally.

He traced a possible line up the wall that offered narrow seams, shallow pockets, and a few wedge-shaped constrictions. Protection would hold here. He selected an assortment of cams, chocks, and nuts, arranging them by size across his harness.

The anchor came first. He found a vertical crack. He placed a #2 cam, tested it with two firm tugs, then backed it up with a chock in a slightly offset seam. Equalized with a sling, the anchor was solid.

He clipped in the VX-3, double-checked the rope path, and then took one final breath through the oxygen mask before pulling it down and letting it hang around his neck.

"Let's finish this."

His first move off the ledge was a high step into a narrow toe pocket. He shifted his weight slowly, found a handhold, and moved. Muscle memory took over. He advanced in slow rhythm—place protection, test it, climb; place, test, climb. Each piece of protection bit solidly into the rock.

Thirty feet up, Adam became short of breath. He paused, one foot balanced on a thin ledge, and placed the mask over his face again. The oxygen flowed, and clarity returned. He pressed on.

At eighty feet, his arms ached. The wall offered no mercy. Just a clean line to be conquered.

He was now one hundred feet up the route. His last chock was seated deep in a flared crack, and he dared not skip the next one. He set a cam into place, gave it a hard yank, and climbed past it.

Finally, his fingers found a flat horizontal slab of stone. His right hand curled over the summit edge, his foot scrambled for purchase, and with a final surge of strength, he hauled himself over the lip, where he removed his harness and pack.

The summit plateau was not what he had expected. He was stunned by everything that wasn't there.

No snowfields.

No drifts.

No glacial crust clinging to the rocks.

Just bare stone—wind-polished and dry as bone.

Adam became dizzy. He returned to his pack and held the oxygen mask to his face. His vision narrowed. Spots formed like stars. And then—everything went still.

The summit was gone. The sky dissolved. There was no sound, only darkness.

He collapsed.

Adam didn't know how long he had been lying there. With his eyes closed, he took a deep breath. It was normal. His chest, though fatigued and sore, didn't labor. The dizziness from earlier had faded. He checked his vitals on his wrist display. His pulse was only slightly elevated. His oxygen saturation was normal. *That's not possible,* he thought.

He opened his eyes and noticed a shimmer. Just above the ground, the air rippled with light. Faint threads of motion coalesced into a form—luminous, shifting, refracting the sky itself. It pulsed softly. Low harmonic tones accompanied its presence.

"I must be dreaming." He said to no one. He gazed at the source of light and sound again as if trying to take hold of a mirage.

Then, he was bombarded by musical tones, some low, some high—all of them chaotic.

He remembered his encounters with the Zenolith. "I mean you no harm," he said softly.

The shimmer steadied, and from within it came a solitary, clear tone that pierced his mind. It was as if a switch had flipped. Slowly now, he heard more tones, each of which carried a message:

"You are seen."

"You are safe."

"You are ready, One Who Walks."

Adam smiled. The shimmering presence was intelligent. His thoughts returned to the mission. If it were intelligent, it needed a name. He sat up, reached into his pack, and pulled out the notebook where Harris had listed the next two species names. "You're not a Tharnak," he said softly. "So, for now… I'll call you *Aerum*."

The presence emitted a gentle series of tones as if to confirm his decision.

He chuckled, a little breathless. "One who walks… guilty as charged."

The song quieted but did not leave. And Adam, sitting on the summit of a world not his own, understood that the mountain was not the end of his journey. It was the beginning of a song.

FORTY

ADAM STAYED on the summit long after the shimmer had faded, unable to move and unwilling to leave the tranquil stillness. Night had fallen. The wind skimmed gently across the stone, but the cold never reached him. He hadn't brought his bivy or sleeping bag. This was meant to be a quick summit attempt. A push to the top and return to base camp. But something had changed.

The presence of the Aerum lingered. It filled the air like breath before speech, enfolding him without touching him. It emitted warmth not as measured by degrees but in how a familiar chord can move the soul.

He lay on the bare stone, his hands beneath his head, his body curled against the open sky—and didn't shiver. He didn't ache. And slowly, sleep overtook him.

He awoke hours later to a glow at the edge of the world.

Thianos was rising.

From the mountaintop, it appeared not as a disc but as a vast curtain of crimson light peeling upward across the horizon. The first rays touched the summit, igniting every ridge and groove of the stone around him in molten garnet and deep rose. The air shimmered with reflected color.

Adam sat up slowly, blinking against the brilliance. He had never seen anything so beautiful.

And then, the shimmer returned. "Seeker," the voice whispered in his mind through a musical note.

He turned toward it. "I'm here."

"Are you willing to find the source?"

"The source of what?" he asked. "The river?"

He heard a deeper tone that seemed an invitation to follow.

He stood and looked at the oxygen tank. He didn't understand why he was breathing normally, but thought: *Maybe I'm not supposed to understand. What if it's a test of some kind?* He left the tank behind. "Lead on," he whispered.

The Aerum shimmered and drifted forward. Adam followed, his boots rubbing softly on the stone as they moved along a narrow ridgeline stretching away from the summit. Below, the planet fell away into deep valleys and folded canyons, awash in magenta. Adam pulled the camera from his pocket and snapped a couple of pictures.

The path narrowed and then twisted as it approached a stone berm some twenty feet high. The trail darted into a cleft—barely wide enough for one person to pass through. He squeezed into it and felt a familiar sensation. *The pull.* It was stronger now—heavier than it had been by the river far below. It pressed into his body like invisible hands, urging him downward.

He made his way between the narrow walls and the cleft opened on the other side. The realm beyond the pass was an amphitheater of light and song. Stones formed elegant arches, and beneath them, there was music. Frequencies beyond speech were woven into the atmosphere like a sacred language.

In the center of the chamber, mist shimmered like breath over water. The pink river began here. It emerged as a shallow basin of glasslike fluid welled from smooth, luminous rock, rising like a melody called forth from silence.

All around the basin, there were dozens of Aerum, shimmering sentient auroras—ribbons of colored light that moved with purpose—drifting among the arches. Their presence pulsed with light and chord, painting the chamber in hues of sapphire, emerald, and amethyst. Each movement left a tonal afterglow—a phrase in a song too ancient to name.

Adam stepped forward slowly, reverently, his boots making no sound. He dropped to his knees beside the basin, overcome. A voice filled his thoughts.

"This is the Source. Of life. Of love."

He felt it then—not just warmth, but *recognition*. As though a melody he had never heard was unfolding inside him, and he knew every note. He lowered his hands into the water. It wasn't cold. It wasn't wet. It was alive.

FORTY-ONE

ADAM REMAINED KNEELING at the edge of the basin, his hands submerged in the luminous, living current of the Source. Then, he heard a voice. It was his own.

"Who am I?"

The question hadn't come from his lips. It arose from his soul. The Source answered with memories that flooded his mind.

A boy sat at a roaring campfire listening to detective stories invented by his father.

A teacher pinned a young boy's drawing on the bulletin board as an example to motivate the class.

A teenager sat beside his mother on the porch at dusk, their quiet laughter mingling with the flashing of fireflies.

A young man stood before a cheering crowd as he received an award for heroism.

Then came other memories.

A boy, curious to learn the power of fire, accidentally burned down his neighbor's barn.

A teenager driving home drunk from a party, ran over his family's dog, killing it.

There was fistfight with his brother.

The woman he almost married, and the painful silence after their last conversation.

The glacier. Rope slithering into the abyss. The scream.

Hundreds of images blurred into one another—failures and victories, mistakes and courageous choices, lies and betrayals. All the moments of his life. The moments he thought had defined him.

He bowed his head. And then, the Source pulsed. "Success and failure do not define you. You are not the sum of your experiences. Long ago, in the stars, your identity was established. It cannot be erased. Not by you. Not by anyone. One Who Walks."

Adam was being taken apart—not broken, but gently untangled. The man he thought he had been was being dismembered. A new image was forming in his mind.

The Source pulsed again, and with it came a wave of feeling unlike anything he'd ever known.

Raw, unconditional love. It hit him like a tsunami and flooded every broken place in his soul, asking for nothing in return. Adam wept—quietly, freely. For the first time in years, he didn't hold back.

FORTY-TWO

THE CORRIDORS of the *Leonidas* were cramped—a twisted maze of riveted bulkheads and exposed conduit—a warship masquerading as a research vessel. The metal groaned faintly with every shift in the wind outside, a reminder that the hull, though sealed, wasn't impervious to the forces at work on Opturius. The crew moved about the ship purposefully, though without any real urgency. There was no enemy to fight. No orbit to maintain. Just a planet full of silence and one man missing in it.

Lieutenant Harrow stood at the central console of the operations bay, his arms folded tight across his chest, watching a cluster of green and yellow lines sweep across a screen.

Communications: active.

Atmospheric sensors: stable.

Life signs external: ambiguous.

"Where the hell are you, Walker?" he asked quietly.

In the corner of the room, Sergeant Vale worked on a bank of communication instruments that had been bolted in place after the ship had launched. He tapped at a screen, frowning. "No offense to Harris," he said, "but we're one glitch away from rerouting this whole operation with duct tape."

"The Major is doing his best," Harrow said. "He didn't sign up to play lab coat."

"None of us did," Vale replied.

A door slid open. Major Harris stepped inside, moved to the center of the room, and stared at the console.

"We're extending the observation window," Harris said. "Walker's gone radio silent but I want to give him more time."

Lieutenant Harrow looked at Harris. "You think he's still climbing?"

"I don't know what he's doing," Harris replied. He stared at the display a moment longer, then turned away. "Keep monitoring. Let me know the second a signal returns."

FORTY-THREE

THE MIST ABOVE ADAM THICKENED. The image of a planet formed in his mind. Sparkling. Opulent. There was a great fracture where there had once been harmony. He saw a war. Cities fallen. The Aerum fleeing, their song stifled. They came to Opturius for one reason. To preserve the song until it could be heard again.

Adam saw himself walking in a new world.

Then, the image faded. He didn't move for a long time. At least he thought it was a long time. He had no idea how long he had been kneeling at the basin. An hour? A day?

The Aerum formed a ring around him, their radiant forms moving in rhythm. A tone—low and resonant—echoed through the chamber.

The Source pulsed once more, and messages filled Adam's mind: "You are not your past. You are not alone. You never were. You are loved. You are needed."

FORTY-FOUR

MAJOR HARRIS SAT ALONE in the dayroom, his fingers steepled beneath his chin, his eyes fixed on the last known coordinates. The moment Adam had stepped through the ship's airlock, Harris developed a low-grade headache. Watching Adam walk out with his pack had set him on edge. He had finally gotten Walker to agree to the mission, but now he wondered if he had sent him to his death.

Harris rubbed his eyes and reached for his tablet. He pulled up Adam's psych profile, skimming lines he knew by heart. The glacier. The suicide attempt.

He closed the file. None of that mattered now. What mattered was the mountain—and whether Adam could face it without losing himself. He looked around the room at the bare walls, save for Adam's drawing of the mountain.

He hadn't expected radio contact, but the silence gnawed at him. He leaned back in the chair and rubbed his temples. Either the man was still up there…

Or he wasn't.

He pulled up the ship's sensor logs again, skimming for anomalies—power fluctuations, atmospheric surges, ground tremors. One spike stood out. A localized pressure dip, too sharp for a storm, too contained for tectonics.

That had been three nights ago, right around the time the monitors went quiet. He stared at the data, trying not to let his imagination fill in the blanks.

So, he sat. And he waited. And for the first time since the mission began, Harris prayed.

Adam awoke to the sound of the Aerum singing. Here, time did not move. There was no sun overhead. No rising or setting of light. The sky had no clouds, nor stars. Just a gentle, perpetual glow that bathed the mountaintop in shades of carmine and rose. The Source—liquid and living—flowed like a luminous artery, pulsing with life.

Adam sat near the edge of the glowing stream, his legs folded beneath him, his hands resting loosely in his lap. His boots had long since been set aside. The stone beneath his feet felt warm. Every few minutes—though he no longer measured things in minutes—the Source would shimmer with a subtle surge. Like breath. Like joy.

The Aerum hovered above the stream's edge, rising and drifting like currents of air. They never approached Adam directly, but their presence enfolded the summit.

He had stopped asking questions. There was nothing to do here. And he felt no urge to leave. He had waited for visions. For instruction. For another task. But none came. Only words, softly impressed on his soul. Not often. And never with demand.

"You are not your failures."

"You are not what they said."

"You were never abandoned."

Each message came like rain to dry soil, reminding him of what he had forgotten—and imparting what he never knew.

He did not respond. There was no need. His presence was answer enough. He rested. And as he did, the ache of his past slowly faded—not by erasure, but by irrelevance. His past—tragic and traumatic—had lost its voice.

At one point, he lay back against the rock, staring up into the glowing sky, his arms spread wide, his breathing slow.

"Is this death?" he had asked, not expecting an answer.

The light pulsed in response. "No. This is life without fear."

FORTY-FIVE

ADAM LINGERED AT THE SUMMIT, the glow of the Source reflected in his eyes. The quiet hum of the Aerum encircled him like a choir, drifting inside the chamber.

What are they doing here?

He blinked. *What am I doing here?*

Distantly, he remembered the mission. The base camps. His excitement to reach the summit. He remembered Harris.

Crap.

"He probably thinks I'm dead."

Adam knew he couldn't stay here forever. *You are needed.* The words echoed softly in his memory. Adam didn't think it referred specifically to Harris, but he knew Harris was counting on him. He looked around the chamber. The soft mist swirled across the glowing basin. The liquid within it continued to rise—not spilling, not overflowing—just giving. He leaned forward again to watch it. Just to be close to it. That's when the change came.

The tones around him shifted. The light of the Aerum dimmed slightly, and their motion grew still. Adam understood the change as a signal. He sat up straighter, alert, without fully knowing why.

Then a voice spoke. "Your time here is short."

"Why?" he asked.

"A change has arrived."

He stood slowly, exerting effort against the downward pull. "What kind of change?"

"They are coming."

Adam turned in place, scanning the amphitheater as though expecting to see someone—or something emerge. But the Aerum didn't move. They remained suspended in the mist, their lights dimmer now, like stars behind a veil of cloud.

He stepped back from the basin.

"Who's coming?" There was no answer. But the feeling intensified.

The Source pulsed once—softly but with finality. Adam felt the shift in his body. The warmth that had kept him during his time on the summit was still present, but it no longer cradled him. The peace was still there, but it was receding.

"Am I in danger?" he asked.

The voice returned. "No. But you must go."

His pulse quickened. He crouched and put on his boots. He paused for one last glance at the basin that had been his source of comfort, then turned and began walking toward the cleft in the rock. The Aerum moved with him. As he passed through the narrow threshold, he felt their final presence invade his thoughts.

"What you have received, you must carry forward. What you have seen, you must remember."

And then, as the light of Thianos filtered back into view, Adam emerged onto the summit ridge.

FORTY-SIX

THE WIND on the summit ridge tore at Adam's jacket as he began his descent. He rappelled down to the ledge below, switched to the next anchor, and continued down. Above him, the summit receded into the growing light of Thianos. Below, the route wound down between jagged ridgelines and narrow shelves. He paused occasionally to check his anchors and gear.

Halfway between the summit and base camp two, he stopped. Not far from the mountain, a storm was materializing. At first, it appeared as a smear of darkness across the red sky. But as he watched, it thickened, blossomed, and moved—a wall of shifting light and shadow crackling with energy. Flashes of blue, green, and violet flickered across a sky already stained with blood and fire. Adam's heart sank. The storm was moving toward the mountain.

A low hum rose from the land itself. Adam quickened his pace. By the time he reached base camp two, the wind was fierce. The gusts were sharp enough to cause him to stagger. The once-still air now howled through the rocks like a living thing. He ducked beneath the overhang where he had stored his gear, dropping his pack and crouching against the back wall of the shallow alcove. He clipped a quickdraw to his harness and one of the bolts.

As soon as he did, the storm hit. The sky went black. A sudden pulse of magnetized air swept over the mountain like a tidal wave. Sparks bounced along the face of the stone. The ledge vibrated beneath him as thunder boomed—not from the sky, but from within the mountain itself, as if something ancient and buried had turned in its sleep.

Wind screamed across the ridge, carrying particles of glowing dust and thin ribbons of light that flashed like plasma. The storm raged, tearing across the rock, shaking loose fragments that skittered down the slopes like fleeing insects.

Adam pressed his body tightly against the rock. His heart pounded. The shaking intensified. Stone groaned beneath him. He closed his eyes and tried to breathe. But the storm had gotten inside him. Fear gripped him. The wind roared through his mind as much as through the terrain, and for a moment, he thought the mountain might crack in half. *This is it,* he thought. *This could actually be it.*

And then—he remembered.

You are not alone.

The words washed over him. The Source was still with him. Still *in* him.

He inhaled slowly amidst the chaos. The fear didn't vanish—but it lost its grip. The mountain still shook, but it no longer felt hostile. The wind still screamed, but he could hear something beneath it now—something steady.

A pulse.

He pressed his palm to the rock beside him. It was vibrating. Singing in its own way. He closed his eyes and began counting breaths. He knew the storm would pass; he just needed to weather it and come out in one piece. He willed himself and the ledge to remain strong.

And as quickly as it had come, the fury faded. The sky lightened. The wind slowed. The groaning of the mountain gave way to silence. When Adam finally emerged from under the ledge, the storm was retreating across the ridges like a living shadow, crackling faintly as it dissolved into the eastern sky.

FORTY-SEVEN

THE FIRST ALERT came as a flicker in the ship's lighting. A fractional drop in cabin pressure followed. They were anomalies that autocorrect in under a second—unless the source is external. Sergeant Vale noticed it first. "Bridge to engineering. We're registering a flux event."

Chief Engineer Schmidt's voice came back over comms. "Confirmed. Planetary-wide disturbance originating in the southern hemisphere."

"Severity?" Vale asked.

Schmidt hesitated. "Off the charts. Might be a coronal mass ejection—planetary scale. Surface EM saturation is rising exponentially."

Vale stood from his console. "Where's Walker?"

Major Harris appeared behind him like a shadow. "I don't know."

"Should we prepare for evacuation?" Corporal Rodriguez asked.

"No," Harris said sharply.

"Then what do we do?"

Harris stared at the console. "We wait."

FORTY-EIGHT

THE STORM HAD PASSED, but Opturius was not the same. Adam moved across the plateau, descending from the high base camp under a sky that had begun to settle into uneasy stillness. Where once there had been clear switchbacks and a familiar form to the terrain, now there was upheaval. The mountain had shifted. Slabs of stone lay cracked and overturned like scattered tablets. A new river had been formed that roared down the mountainside. Patches of vegetation had been ripped free and tossed downslope. Dust hung in the air, refracting the light of Thianos into strange hues. With the usual navigation markers no longer present, Adam made the mental adjustments and plotted a course to the ship. When he reached the final ridge and saw the familiar canyon below, relief passed through him.

Adam continued and at last, entered the rim of the canyon. The trail of footprints had been erased by the storm. He knew the approximate location of the ship in relation to the canyon walls and eventually located the hatch.

He went inside, dust-covered, shaggy-bearded, and exhausted. He dropped his pack with a thud and leaned back against the wall. He looked ten pounds lighter. Harris had been waiting in the dayroom.

"I made it," Adam said.

"No shit," Harris fired back.

Adam gave a weak smile, then chuckled. "Didn't think I would, huh?"

"I had a bag packed," Harris replied. "I was going to come find you and kick your ass for making me hike to the top of this godforsaken rock."

Adam laughed. "Sounds like fun. Maybe next time."

"I gave you orders for a five day summit attempt. Not a two-week Caribbean cruise."

"It took three days for my body to acclimatize. I broke a couple ribs on a fall and had to rehab. Then I got buried in a sandstorm. And that was before I reached the summit."

Harris stared at him. "Did you lose the radio or just forget how to use it?"

"I tried to contact you after the fall, but no one heard me. Then the wind carried the radio down the mountainside."

Harris finally motioned toward the chairs. "Well, if you're going to go rogue, you might as well tell me what the hell you found up there."

Adam collapsed in the chair. Harris sat opposite him.

Adam looked up. "Can I get something to eat first? I'm starving."

Harris nodded and left through the door opposite the bedroom. He came back with some jerky, an apple, and a glass of water.

Adam downed the water and gnawed at the jerky. After a few bites, he took a deep breath. "You won't believe what happened."

Harris grabbed a piece of the jerky and tore a chunk off with his teeth. "Try me."

And so, Adam told him.

He described the days spent waiting for dizziness and nausea to subside, the fall that left him bleeding, the cold, snowless summit plateau, the blackout from lack of oxygen, and the shimmer in the air that was formless yet alive. "We have a new intelligence. I'm calling it the Aerum." He described its appearance, its harmonics, and the way it sang without voice.

Harris listened.

Adam watched Harris's reaction, then leaned forward dramatically. "There's more."

Harris shook his head. "Of course there is."

Adam described the passage through the narrow cleft, the amphitheater, the basin, and the Source surrounded by dozens of Aerum. He told of the peace he'd found, the memories he'd seen, the messages whispered to him, and the all-consuming love he had encountered.

"I would have stayed longer, but the Source said I had to leave. And it said something else."

"What else did it say?"

"It said 'they are coming.'"

"And you believe all of this was real?"

Adam stopped mid-chew and glared at him. "I didn't find any wild mushrooms or hemp out there. Of course it was real. It's the most real thing I've ever experienced."

"Fair enough."

They sat in silence for a moment. Then Harris asked, almost casually, "Any idea what 'they are coming' means?"

"We already know Opturius is expecting visitors."

"Visitors," Harris said quietly. "That's putting it nicely."

"Anything I need to know, or is this a secret squirrel thing?"

"The only thing you need to know for now is that we're not the only ones interested in this planet."

Adam began devouring the apple. It was a Fuji, his favorite. He wondered if Harris somehow knew that. He seemed to know everything else about him. "The trip back down," he said. "The storm tore everything up. Water flows were rerouted. Massive stones were overturned. It was violent. But beautiful in a way. In the middle of it, when I thought I might die, I remembered what the Source had told me... I'm not alone."

Harris studied him. Then he gave a slow nod as if some part of him understood—even if he couldn't say so out loud. "You're referring to this as 'the Source,'" he said. "We've been instructed to use standardized nomenclature for all intelligent life forms."

Adam stared at the bottle of pink fluid that still sat on the desk where he had left it before his trip to the summit. "When the Aerum asked me to visit the origin of the river, they called it "The Source."

"Our system refers to it as Hydrological Entity Alpha," Harris said. "H.E.A. for short."

Adam shook his head. "You can't name a sacred being like it's a brand of bacon."

"Tell that to the guys upstairs. They like their labels neat."

Adam picked up the bottle and turned it slowly in his hand. "It didn't feel like a body of water. Not really. It was... watching."

Harris gave a slow nod. "I don't doubt that."

"So, you agree that it's intelligent, not just a puddle of primordial goo?"

Harris shrugged. "It's your report. It's not my job to override your observations. I'm just here to pass along information. But if it's intelligent, the system needs a handle. You think 'the Source' is any better?"

"It's not a handle," Adam said quietly. "It's an admission."

"Of what?"

"You name what you understand. You bow down to what you can't."

"It's funny," Harris finally said, "we keep thinking we're the superior species doing the observing."

Adam anticipated his thought, "Maybe we're the ones under the microscope."

Harris leaned forward and tapped the bottle with his knuckle. A dull sound echoed in the silence. "You think it's aware of us... *here*?"

Adam nodded. "I don't think it ever stopped being aware."

Harris drew back his hand. They stared at the bottle. It didn't change, but the room felt warmer.

Adam stood, pushing his chair back gently. "I need to clean up." As he walked toward his room, the pink fluid in the bottle moved slightly, shifting toward the sound of his footsteps.

FORTY-NINE

THE SHIP'S LOUNGE, a repurposed storage room, had become the crew's unofficial meeting ground. Half a dozen video monitors covered one wall. Corporal Rodriguez's eyes were glued to one screen where she watched but did not hear Harris interview Adam. The video feed had no audio.

Rodriguez watched Adam as he walked from the dayroom to his bed. "Is it just me, or does he seem different?"

Lieutenant Harrow sipped tea from a lukewarm thermos. "He saw something up there."

"You can see it in his eyes," Sergeant Vale added, seated on a wooden crate nearby.

Rodriguez turned. "What do you mean?"

"They're still his eyes. Same color. Same shape. But the way he looked at Harris…" Vale shook his head. "It's like he sees something no one else does."

"Or maybe something we do," Harrow added, "but we've spent our lives pretending we didn't."

"You know," Vale said, "we keep thinking he was up there climbing his ass off, trying to survive all those ridiculous conditions, and that freak storm that should have killed *anything* on that mountain, and he just somehow magically walks back into the ship safe and sound. It doesn't add up."

"He's a survivor," Rodriguez said.

"I don't doubt that," Vale replied, "but what if he got help?"

"From what?" Rodriguez asked.

"There was a weird signal just before Adam returned to the ship. The instruments picked it up." Vale said. "Some kind of resonance, almost like sonar bouncing off the crust. Never seen anything like it."

"You think it was from the summit?" Rodriguez asked.

"I think something pinged Adam's position. Whatever it is, I think it's tracking him."

FIFTY

THE DOOR HARRIS used to enter the dayroom stood open. For weeks, Adam's world had been the same sterile room, the same bed, and the same unyielding routine. But now, Harris stood beside him, arms crossed, grinning.

"You've earned a look behind the curtain," Harris said.

Adam stepped through the doorway leading to a part of the ship he had never seen. The corridor was narrow, dark, and utilitarian. The air carried the scents of hand lotion and deodorant. They turned a corner and passed through an open door to the ship's lounge. A woman with short, black hair looked up from her seat.

"Holy hell," Corporal Rodriguez said, rising to her feet. "It's him."

A few heads turned. A man with grease-stained sleeves leaned around a bulkhead, blinking twice. "The Walker himself."

Adam offered a hesitant smile. "Didn't know I had a fan club."

"You don't," Rodriguez replied with a grin. "We took bets on whether we'd ever talk to you in person. Vale owes me ten."

A bald man at the back groaned. "Guys, that's not Walker," Vale said. "It's a robot. Double or nothing he doesn't have a pulse." Laughter filled the space—brief and genuine.

Harris gave a nod to the crew. "This is Adam Walker. The reason we're still here. Shake his hand or keep working—your choice."

The tension eased. Hands were offered. Names were exchanged. Someone offered Adam a cup of coffee that didn't taste like rehydrated dirt. Adam felt tangibly human.

After a few minutes, Harris gestured for him to follow. They made their way to the rear chamber, past a room with crates marked *Survey Equipment*, past the cryo-bay he hadn't yet asked about. Harris opened the door to his bunk room. They stepped inside a room only slightly larger than a closet.

"You're out there, sleeping on the ground, so I thought I'd show you my bachelor pad."

Adam laughed softly. Then he turned to Harris. "Why now? Why show me all this?"

Harris leaned against the door. "Because you've seen things we never will. You've met the soul of this planet. And I figured it was time you met the machine that got you here—and the people still hoping you'd make it back."

Adam looked around, the overhead lights reflecting faintly in his eyes.

"Thanks," he said.

"For what?"

"For reminding me I'm not alone."

"You never were."

They stood there together—two men caught in the narrow space between the beginning of the journey and the return.

FIFTY-ONE

MAJOR HARRIS and Adam met the following morning in the dayroom to discuss the next phase of the mission.

"I've been thinking," Adam said. "If the Aerum and the Zenolith inhabit different regions, there are probably others."

Harris sipped his coffee. "You think the whole planet's populated?"

"We've only seen the first layer. And I think that storm was surgical. Like it was meant to open something."

Harris set down his coffee. "I'm not tracking you. Care to elaborate?"

"I have a directive, remember? At the river. The message was clear. You must go there. The river knows more about this planet than we do. It wants me to explore whatever is below the plateau. We get hit with a storm that rearranges the entire geology of the planet. What if the storm opened a new route that allows us to explore what we couldn't get to before?"

"The storm did more than just rearrange the geology of the planet; it damaged the ship. Exploring the region below the plateau would best be done by relocating the ship. I'm not sure if that's possible now."

"You don't need to move the ship. I can get there."

"You realize that we don't know what's down there. You step off the edge, and you're on your own."

"It can't be any worse than what I went through to get to the summit and back."

"I'll give you credit. That was some slick work getting to the summit. But returning, you had gravity on your side. It was all downhill. You go below the plateau and you may not be able to get back up."

"I'm not going to throw myself into a canyon," he said. "I'll stick to the edge. Do a terrain survey. Identify a potential descent point and make sure there's a way back up. That's it—for now."

Major Harris pretended to fiddle with his tablet. He stared at Adam, the soldier's mask slipping just enough to reveal a softer man beneath. "I don't want to lose you," he said. "Not to this place. Not to that river. Not to whatever's pulling you."

Adam's voice softened. "That's just it. I'm not being pulled." He stood, stretched the ache out of his shoulders, then looked Harris in the eye. "I'm being called."

"Pulled, called, same thing."

"It's different and you know it."

Harris rubbed a hand over his jaw, then gave a short nod. "Fine. You've got one day. Out at dawn. Back by nightfall. No heroics. No descents. You're scouting. That's it."

"Understood."

"If you're not back by sundown," Harris said, standing with him, "I'm coming to find you myself. And when I do, you'll wish you had come back in time."

"Don't worry Mom, I'll be home for supper."

FIFTY-TWO

THE PLATEAU STRETCHED SOUTHWARD like the end of a world. The land flattened for miles, then crumbled into a vast, jagged drop—an escarpment that seemed to fall forever. Adam hiked southward with a renewed sense of purpose. The wind kicked up dust in swirling spirals. Each step across the barren crust of the plateau felt like trespass, as if the land were watching.

The air, the light, the very mood of the terrain shifted. He crested a low rise and stopped fifty yards from the precipice. Below, a vast desert stretched out reaching for the horizon—red dunes, cracked rock, sweeps of ash-colored sand broken by mesas and ravines. To the west, tall, slender spires rose from the desert floor. In the middle of it all was a river. Wide, dark, and slow. It cut through the land like it had carved the planet itself, terminating at the sea far in the distance.

Adam walked to the cliff's edge, his eyes scanning for movement, landmarks, anything that might suggest sentience.

Nothing.

He pulled his notebook and a stub of pencil from his pack and began sketching the topography. He traced the snaking river, then noted the escarpment's contours. Some of the terrain was sheer vertical walls, but not all. To the southwest, a long ridge descended in stepped shelves, broken by outcrops and ledges.

He saw a boulder field below a ledge that covered perhaps a thousand feet from top to bottom. There wasn't a trail, and it wasn't exactly a staircase, but it looked like it could be traversed without ropes or mechanical aid. It didn't extend as far as the valley floor, but it would get him close.

He focused his field scope, tracing a potential descent path from shelf to shelf and across the boulder field, and scribbled notes. It was steep but navigable. Technical in a couple of places. Risky—but not suicidal.

That's the route.

Adam scanned the rim. A small patch of stone jutted out from the main bluff. It was shaded and protected from the wind. The perfect cache site. He made a mental note of the site's location, then returned to the ship.

FIFTY-THREE

ADAM TORE a page from his notebook. It was a drawing of the desert below the plateau. He taped it on the blank wall between his bathroom and the doorway.

Harris watched silently from his chair in the dayroom. *He's finally making this prison his home.*

Adam entered the dayroom and took a seat at the desk, then opened the notebook.

"What did you find?" Harris asked.

"There's a slope that leads to a narrow ledge system to the southwest, and there's a boulder field. From there, I think I can descend to the desert floor—but I'll need to leave ropes fixed along at least five pitches."

"How far down?"

"Hard to say for sure, but I estimate four thousand feet of total elevation loss. Multiple sheer faces. And the climb back up won't be fast."

"So, a one-way route until proven otherwise."

"Not necessarily. As long as I have fixed ropes, I can get back. I'll need multiple static lines, anchors, food, water, and desert gear for the bottom. And a few redundancies."

"Another base camp?"

"I have a location picked out where I can stash gear."

"You know this isn't a survey mission. We're in a planetary diplomatic posture. Every time you go out, it's a political risk."

"Which is why we need to know if something lives down there."

Harris sighed. "Five days."

Adam shook his head. "You can't be serious."

"You have five days," Harris repeated.

Adam nodded. "Fine."

"I'm serious. I've had enough MIA reports for one deployment."

Adam smiled. "I'll pack light."

FIFTY-FOUR

THE NEXT DAY, Adam stood beside the desk in the dayroom filling his pack. He double-checked the gear to make sure he hadn't forgotten anything. Major Harris stood by the entry door of the ship. He handed Adam a radio. "This time, don't lose it."

Adam stowed the radio in the pack. "Yes, sir."

He turned and stepped out into the light of Thianos, walking south, observing the usual plants and the occasional shimmer of insect wings. His footfalls raised small clouds of red dust. By mid-afternoon, he had reached the edge. He slipped the pack off his shoulders. One by one, he emptied rope bags and bundles of nylon webbing onto the ground, then placed them in the shade offered by a pile of rocks. He covered them with a tarp and secured it with a few stones. It wouldn't pass for invisible, but it would survive until tomorrow. Then, he turned and made the long trek back across the plateau.

The next morning, Adam rose before first light and left the safety of the ship. The journey back to the edge of the plateau took longer with the added weight. Sweat clung to his back, and his thighs ached. When he reached the gear cache, everything was still in place. He began moving the webbing and rope bags to the location where he would rappel. The plan was to secure enough rope and webbing for anchors to the outside of his pack, with the intention of leaving it all in place.

By midday, everything was staged. He sat at the rim of the world, his hands resting on the warm stone, and stared down into the wilderness that waited below. He felt small. A gentle warmth rose in his chest. He closed his eyes, breathed in, and exhaled fully. It was time.

Adam wrapped a nylon runner around a large boulder and backed up the anchor with an identical setup on a second rock. He joined them with an equalizing runner and donned his harness, then prepared to rappel. The edge of the plateau fell away beneath his boots like the lip of a forgotten world.

Below stretched a sun-scorched wilderness—a mosaic of red rock, shifting sands, jagged ridgelines, and fractured shelves. He lowered himself down onto a broad ledge, making sure his footing was solid. There was no path forged before him, no guarantee that the route he chose would take him to the desert floor.

The next section began with a long traverse across a tilted slab—a slick stone fractured by ancient tectonic scars. Six hundred feet in, the next vertical wall came into view: a drop of eighty feet straight down. Once again, he secured a nylon sling to a large boulder, tied off a length of rope to it, and then tossed the free end of the rope over the edge. He looped a bight of rope through his figure eight, secured it to his harness with a carabiner, locked the gate, and descended.

At the bottom, he removed the figure eight from his harness and stowed it. The rope stayed behind, fluttering like a thread in the wind.

He continued scrambling across slanted slabs of soft sedimentary stone. Two more vertical pitches followed—one over seventy feet and the next closer to ninety. Each wall seemed more unstable than the last. Stones crumbled underfoot. Wind scraped across his goggles. His descent was a calculated sacrifice—leaving rope, height, and options behind him.

The series of stepped ledges gave way to a long slope of boulders piled on top of one another. Adam hopped from one boulder to another, gradually descending the talus slope. With every move, he had to carefully counterbalance the weight of his pack.

Having left the boulder field, he located another assemblage of ledges and made his way lower. His legs burned when he reached the last wall. This was the final drop. A vertical cliff nearly 150 feet high.

Adam crouched near the edge and peered down. The red desert basin yawned below him. He pulled a coil of rope from its bag and dropped it near his feet.

With no suitable boulder nearby to tie off to, the best anchor point was a vertical crack in the wall above him. He pulled out an assortment of cams, hexes, and nuts from his pack and examined the crevice. He inserted a hex into it, attached a nylon runner, then pulled on it. It shifted, then wedged. The rock here was soft and flaky, and the hex might pull out under load. He pulled the drill Harris had given him from his pack. He tapped the stone and found a firm pocket just above the hex and installed a bolt, linking both points with an equalizing runner to distribute the load. He tested the system with his body weight. No obvious flex. The bolt was clean. The hex was holding.

He tied in, double-checked his knot and carabiner gate, and backed into the void. The rock face was smooth. His gloved hands warmed from friction as his speed increased. He was descending too fast. With twenty feet left to go, he applied firm braking pressure to slow his descent and came to an abrupt stop. A sharp *snap* echoed like a gunshot, and the rope shifted. The hex had pulled out of the crack. An instant later, the remaining bolt took the shock load and tore free from the crumbling wall.

Adam felt the sickening sensation of free-fall as he dropped to the desert floor. His shoulder hit the ground first, followed by a jolt that sent pain spiking through his chest. He screamed, clutching his left arm.

Instantly, the memory returned of the time he dislocated his shoulder on a climbing trip in Utah. "Not again." He rolled onto his side to prevent further movement. "Okay," he whispered. "That's enough excitement for one day."

He looked around, then dragged himself into the shadow of the wall and sat upright, cradling the injured shoulder. He knew what he had to do next. He also knew he wasn't doing it sober. With his right hand, he loosened the straps of his pack enough to slide it off his back.

He opened a side pocket on the pack and retrieved a metal flask.

He held the flask up to the sky, squinted theatrically, and lipped into character. With a drawled Southern accent, he bellowed, "Wyatt... I do declare, I have never imbibed of the devil's elixir for reasons merely recreational."

He twisted off the cap and took a long, burning swallow. The taste of 15-year single malt scotch filled his mouth like fire and oak and salvation.

"However, I have, on occasion, been known to resort to such intoxicating beverages purely for medicinal purposes."

He grinned, swayed slightly, and added, "You understand, of course."

He took another long swig. Then one more for courage.

He recapped the flask then sat against the wall and let it take effect.

"Why the hell do you need scotch? This isn't a party, Walker," Harris had said.

Adam was insistent on acquiring a pint of booze before he left. "What if I lacerate my wrist? It's a *great* antiseptic. And if I have to cut my leg off, I can use it for anesthesia. Oh... and if I run out of fuel, I can use it as an accelerant for starting a fire. It's a Swiss army knife in a bottle."

Harris scowled, but he relented. "If you fall down that Godforsaken cliff because you're *drunk*, I'm leaving your damn body out there to become a fossil."

Adam saluted. "Aye aye, cappin'."

Feeling the welcome blur of numbness kick in, Adam looked for an anchor point. A crack in the wall offered to assist with the procedure. He retrieved the hex that had pulled out of the wall above, still attached to the rope that lay strewn across the desert. He inserted it into the crack, and pulled on it. It didn't move. He pulled an accessory cord from his pack, looped it around his injured arm in a prusik knot, and connected it to the hex with a carabiner. He took a steadying breath, then placed one foot against the wall, leaned back, and pushed. There was a sickening *pop*, a flash of white-hot pain, and then—relief.

He dropped to the ground, gasping. He lay there for half an hour, while his beleaguered brain reconnected to his battered body. The sun blazed brightly in the firmament when he finally staggered away from the wall and surveyed his surroundings.

FIFTY-FIVE

ADAM MOVED SLOWLY through the desert basin, the heat proving to be an unrelenting source of torment. The sand shifted with each step, whispering against the soles of his boots. Every breath was dry fire. He adjusted the makeshift sling on his injured arm—a rigged support tied against his chest. The shoulder throbbed, but he'd endured worse.

The desert around him was not flat, but fluted—an immense geological tapestry of wind-scoured channels, separating tall, slender, stone spires. The columns rose like teeth from the desert floor—hundreds of them scattered across the landscape. Some stood alone, regal and forbidding, while others formed loose clusters as if grown from invisible roots. The tallest reached nearly to the level of the plateau from which Adam had come, casting long shadows across the basin like sundials forgotten by time.

Adam observed the nearest pillar—a column of blood-red stone, faceted like a crystal, each face catching and refracting the light. Even from a distance, the surface shimmered with a luster unlike anything he'd seen on Earth. There were no seams. No erosion scars. Only a few etchings—weather-worn but still visible.

He whispered aloud, "*Karethite.*"

It was a name Harris had once mentioned when describing alien mineral cores—materials that seemed not just engineered, but grown under conditions no Earthbound scientist could reproduce. Adam didn't know who had coined the term. But the name suited these sentinels.

As he moved between the spires, he considered possible routes, studying angles, cracks, and overhangs. Some of the smaller spires could probably be free climbed—if he could find natural features to use as holds. *The larger ones might require bolting,* he thought. Climbing one of the columns would give him a vantage point where he could map the convergence of canyons, maybe even spot other lifeforms.

He paused near a spire, removed his glove, and placed a hand against its base. It was cool. Unusually so. Not in the way stone should be after a night in the desert—but as though it rejected heat altogether.

Adam backed away and resumed walking, weaving between the pillars. The further he walked westward, the more numerous the columns became. Some leaned slightly toward each other, as though conferring with one another. Others bore strange scars—burns, fractures, or weathering patterns that resembled symbols. Then, he found a natural amphitheater formed by a semicircle of these towers, their tops twisted inward, forming a nearly solid arc of stone at the center.

He stopped there. *This place has design.*

The semicircle seemed as good a place as any to set up camp. It was sheltered from the wind and provided protection from potential predators. He unrolled his bivy sack, then unpacked his food, water, and stove. He heated a mug of water, rehydrated a package of food, and ate in the shade of the spires.

As night came, the desert's heat dissipated quickly, leaving Adam chilled in his bivy. Exhausted from the descent, he dropped off to sleep.

FIFTY-SIX

ADAM WOKE JUST BEFORE DAWN. He sipped a cup of coffee while heating the water for his morning meal. He made quick work of breakfast, stowed his gear, and headed east, in what he reckoned was the direction of the river. He hoped to scout the land before the worst heat of the day set in.

Moving eastward, the number of stone spires decreased. They were numerous to the west, but nearly absent here. Then, Adam saw an unusual specimen. It caught his attention for two reasons:

First, it didn't match the others. While most of the Karethite columns rose in smooth shafts of unbroken symmetry, this one was twisted as if caught mid-turn, like an ice-skater frozen in stone. Second, it sang.

He noticed it after crossing a dry gully that divided the cluster of towers near the center of the basin. The wind here was sharper, funneled through the gully's walls. But as he neared the base of this particular spire, the whistle from passing wind shifted into something purer—notes, harmonics, vibrations that hovered on the edge of musical structure. At first, he thought it was his imagination. Then he removed his gloves and touched the stone.

A low vibration rippled through his hand. He leaned closer and rested his head against the column. A tone resonated in his skull, like a single note played on a crystal instrument. He stepped back and stared at the tower, uncertain what to make of it.

The spire rose perhaps 100 feet above the footing, its base was wide, flaring into a foundation of fractured rock. Its surface shimmered slightly—not reflective, but self-luminous, casting the faintest blue halo into the morning air. He walked around its base, noting a raised spiral ridge that ran from foot to crown.

Adam looked eastward, then pulled out his field scope and surveyed the horizon. A dark line was visible that cut through the terrain from north to south.

The river.

Twenty minutes of walking and Adam was at the river's edge. He noted the familiar downward pull and the feeling that he was being observed. Standing beside the flow of pink water, he closed his eyes. "You said I needed to come here."

He waited, but sensed nothing.

Well, he thought, *I followed orders.*

Adam's attention was again drawn to the spires. They intrigued him and needed further exploration. He was certain the puzzle pieces would come together, given enough time. He began walking west, and soon, he was surrounded by them. Thianos was rising, and the heat grew intense. While exploring an area along the cliffs that was sheltered from the sun, he saw something move at the edge of his vision. Then came a sound, like stones knocking together in rhythm.

He froze. Across the sand, a couple of hundred yards away near a spire, something shifted. At first, it looked like a boulder—then it moved. It was massive, with legs like tree trunks. The creature's body was low-slung, with thick, segmented armor that looked like it had grown from the rock itself. Its surface was dull, textured like scorched sandstone, but alive, rippling, and flexing.

Two more creatures rose behind it. Adam knew the name that was next on the list.

Tharnak.

The three creatures stood still, their legs braced like stone pillars, their broad armored bodies hunched against the wind. They had no eyes as far as he could tell. No visible mouths. Just sensory fronds curling from their plated skulls, quivering in the air like antennae. Then, they turned toward him.

Adam felt the ground vibrate beneath him. The lead Tharnak stepped forward, its six massive legs moving with fluid precision. The fronds on its head undulated slowly. Adam steadied himself. His instincts screamed at him to run. But something deeper told him to hold still.

He closed his eyes and reached out with his thoughts as he had with the Aerum. He shaped his message not in words but intent: *I seek to understand.*

One of the Tharnak struck the ground with a single massive leg —*thoom*. A low hum vibrated through the sand and into Adam's feet and spine. He sensed there was a message, but he couldn't discern its meaning. He cautiously stepped forward, raising one hand—palm out.

"I mean you no harm," he said aloud, though he knew the words were irrelevant. He let the emotion carry the weight of the message: peace and respect.

The lead Tharnak tilted its armored head and tapped the ground twice, with one of its legs emitting vibrations. Adam felt them. He closed his eyes again, waiting for a message, but no meaning was discernible.

The Tharnak raised one leg and brought it down in a slow, deliberate stomp.

Thoom.

The ground trembled. Dust danced in low spirals around Adam's boots.

Another stomp, slightly off-rhythm.

Thoom—pause—thoom.

Adam narrowed his eyes. It wasn't random. There was a pattern to it. He dropped to one knee and placed his palm against the ground. The aftershocks still pulsed through the canyon floor, traveling up his arm, steady and deliberate, almost like drumbeats.

The Tharnak shifted again and began walking toward him.

Adam stood and backed against the wall, keeping his hands open and visible. The beast slowed as it neared, until it stood less than twenty feet away, its fronds swiveling to track him. Then, it did something unexpected.

The Tharnak extended one of its fronds—slender, flexible, and covered in a fine lattice of cilia. But instead of brushing against Adam, it reached downward and pressed against a flat slab of stone.

Adam crouched and placed his hand on the stone. He felt a pattern. Not just pressure or rhythm but something deeper: layered vibrations pulsing in a sequence.

He closed his eyes and pressed both hands flat.

Low-high-low... pause... high-high-low.

It wasn't noise. It was meaning. A kind of language he didn't know how to translate.

The frond withdrew.

Then, the Tharnak shifted its posture, lowering its massive torso toward the ground—awkwardly at first. As it settled into a kind of squat, Adam saw it then: a narrow seam on its underside, just behind the forelimbs. As the plates of chitin flexed outward, a soft membrane was exposed. Adam stared at a pale, glistening ventral organ rimmed with short, bristled fibers.

The gland moved, and a wave of vibration entered him—and with it, came a message: "Why here?"

The Tharnak had sent a key that decoded its language. Adam placed his hand on the ground again, and in his mind, he formed a simple thought:

I want to understand your way of life.

The gland retracted. The Tharnak rose again with glacial dignity, turned, and began moving west. It stopped briefly and waved its frond, as if gesturing for him to follow.

As Adam walked behind the Tharnak across the arid basin, to his left, a patch of long, tapered stalks with translucent, fibrous fronds caught his eye.

Further on, tufts of bristled vine lay half-buried in loose soil, each cluster a sprawl of wiry tendrils tipped with dark violet bulbs. As he brushed past one, the bulbs retracted in unison, vanishing into the vines as though startled.

As they passed a massive spire, to his right, Adam saw motion moving away from him. He turned in time to see a reptilian creature no longer than his forearm, its color blending into the desert. It froze briefly, then bolted, its segmented tail slicing the air like a whip.

The Tharnak continued moving westward until they reached a place where the spires grew together into walls, at last, arriving at a narrow slot canyon. Smooth stone walls rose on either side, glittering with flecks of mineral that caught the light like embedded stars.

Inside the canyon, a stillness lingered. At the far end of the grotto, the lead Tharnak turned abruptly into a passageway not visible to the casual observer. Natural vertical lines on the segmented stone walls mimicked the opening to the passageway—not obvious until one had entered it. Adam gazed at a hidden hollow—a natural shelter shaped by time, heat, and ritual.

The Tharnak stepped aside, leaving space for Adam to enter. He walked through into a chamber that was shallow and dry, filled with the scent of mineral dust. Etchings lined the walls—carved glyphs, abstract but purposeful. Spirals, arcs, and lines arranged in repeating patterns. A form of writing, perhaps. But written by whom?

He dropped his pack and sat against the far wall. His body was wrecked. His shoulder throbbed, his legs ached, and the dust had found its way into every seam of his clothing.

The lead Tharnak entered last and curled its armored frame near the entrance like a guardian monument. The others remained outside.

Night had come, but Adam didn't sleep. He sat in the darkness, breathing. Aching. Thinking.

He was yanked from his thoughts when the Tharnak nearest him extended its frond and touched his face. As vibrations raced across his skull, a vision formed in his mind. A hatchling Tharnak, no larger than a housecat, was stranded near a cliff's edge, screaming in pain. Two adults stood nearby, unmoving. Watching.

The image shifted—rain fell, winds howled, the hatchling struggled alone. Adam wanted to cry out, *Help it! Save it!* But he remained silent.

Then he understood. The lesson wasn't cruelty; it was trial. Survival on Opturius required not intervention but endurance. The hatchling eventually pulled itself to safety. It staggered, limped, and climbed. And when it had reached the other Thank, one of them touched it gently with its fronds.

Not before.

After.

Trust, Adam realized, was not given freely among the Tharnak. It was earned through trial.

The lead Tharnak transmitted another set of vibrations.

We will walk beside you, but we will not carry you.

That was their way. Adam respected it. He looked toward the Tharnak nearest to him. He gave a nod, more to himself than to it. "I won't ask you to carry me," he whispered. Just as the words left his mouth, the lead Tharnak rose and turned deeper into the stone corridor. The others followed. Adam stood and followed them. They entered a tight stone passage. And there—beneath a sloped shelf of overhanging rock—a spring bubbled silently from the canyon floor.

The water was not clear, but pink and had the same color and viscosity as the river.

He watched as the Tharnak approached the pool, one by one. They did not drink in the way animals would. Instead, they knelt—if such a word could apply—lowering their bodies over the spring, letting the liquid absorb into their ventral skin. Their plates hummed faintly, and a subtle glow passed through their inner shells.

Adam understood the significance. This was their only sustenance.

Their lifeline.

Their ritual.

And in their presence, he understood that this place was sacred. Quietly, humbly, he knelt beside the spring and cupped his good hand into the fluid.

It was warm, viscous, and alive. Just like the Source. He touched it to his lips and was overcome by a feeling of acceptance.

An hour later, when the ritual had come to its conclusion, the Tharnak began to leave the sanctuary. Adam followed them to the entrance of the slot canyon. The Tharnak moved further west, deeper into the canyons, seemingly indifferent to his presence. He headed east and returned to his camp, and once there, settled in for the night.

FIFTY-SEVEN

ADAM WAS AWAKE AT DAWN. His shoulder no longer ached, which made him wonder if the pink liquid had healing properties. His ribs and shoulder having healed, he felt another climbing challenge was in order. So, he set out toward the singing spire. It was a short hike from camp. The winds gusted around the base of the spire as he arrived. During his first visit, he had marveled at the way it emitted sound. Now, he was drawn back by an ache, a pull. The pull that worried Harris. The column rose like a blade into the sky, flawless and faceted, its surface smooth but for a single raised ridge running from base to apex. A ridge that begged to be climbed. Adam tapped it with his hammer. *Hard stuff, indeed*, he thought. He didn't want to deface such a marvelous work of art with bolts. But a voice nagged at him, insisting it could be climbed without aid. A fall from more than 30 feet would be the end of him. But he wondered if perhaps the planet had loaded the dice in his favor.

What the hell. You only live once.

Adam laced up his climbing shoes and moved onto the raised ridge. He followed the twist upward. The crystalline surface was unlike anything he'd ever touched. Halfway to the top, he had not yet slipped once.

The spire narrowed, and finally, he reached the top. The uppermost surface wasn't flat. A smooth, shallow depression lay at its center, like a bowl carved by eons of erosive force. Inside the bowl sat a hexagonal stone—some two feet in diameter, its facets were dull from dust and time. Adam knelt beside it. He removed his gloves and brushed away the dust with his hand.

The instant his skin made contact, it pulsed.

A blue glow ignited from within the stone. The pulse spread in waves along the surface of the stone bowl, then shot down the spire's shaft. He stepped back, then turned and watched as the pulse spread from the base and traveled across the desert floor like lightning.

Dozens of other spires—miles away—answered. First one. Then another. It was a network. Each spire illuminated with a matching glow, as if recognizing a long-lost sibling. Adam stood transfixed.

"What the hell is this?" he whispered.

And, as if the spire had been waiting for that very question, Adam fell into a trance.

The world peeled back. Light washed over him—amber, crimson, and sapphire.

From a vantage point that was far above Opturius, he saw the planet as it had once been. A lattice of light from horizon to horizon. Spires glowed like stars upon the surface, connected in geometric symmetry. A chorus of sound—low and sustained—rose from the lights like sacred breath.

The Zenolith were newborn then. He saw them emerge from the bases of the spires like columns of coalesced stone and light. The Aerum moved effortlessly through the sky, between the pillars, singing in harmony with them.

Then came the rupture. A foreign frequency disrupted the harmony. Opturius had been invaded. He could not see by what. He only saw the consequences. The spires fractured. Some exploded. Others dimmed. All fell silent. The Aerum were also silenced, and fled to the mountains. The Zenolith wept in stillness, retreating into solitude.

The song of Opturius had ceased. The planet became quiet. Darkness reigned for an age.

But then—*lightning*.

Adam saw again the great storm he'd survived on the mountain, but this time, from above. Bolts of light struck at the spires. The planet had not been broken beyond repair. It had been waiting for a reboot. The storm reconnected the network. Adam acted as the switch.

Suddenly, the vision dissipated. Adam was back on the spire, disoriented. The stone beside him glowed. He looked out across the desert westward. Light from dozens of spires twinkled in the distance.

FIFTY-EIGHT

FROM HIS PERCH atop the spire, Adam noticed movement in the desert below. Not from the Tharnak—he knew them now. These shapes were unfamiliar. Two creatures circled each other in the open desert. They stood nearly 8 feet in height, their limbs long and jointed in multiple places like walking branches. Their skin was mottled gray, textured like shale. Where eyes might be, they bore dark pits lined with glossy ridges. Their heads ended in sharp crests, and from their backs grew stiff, fin-like protrusions that flicked and spread like threat displays. Then they clashed. One slammed the other with a forelimb that bent at unnatural angles. The second responded with a shriek. It lunged, its claws raking, slashing through its opponent's plated hide.

The first creature staggered, liquid spilling from a gash across its abdomen. It let out a cry. No mercy followed. The second drove its claw through the other's torso. Then it stood motionless as the dying creature slumped, spasming once before collapsing entirely. The surviving creature scrambled south and was soon out of view.

Adam remained atop the spire after the survivor had left. He hadn't been seen. Or if he had, he'd been ignored. When he was certain the threat was gone, he descended the spire and hiked west toward camp.

He stopped at one point, crouching near a cluster of desert flora that looked strangely familiar. It reminded him of a yucca—except that instead of dagger-like leaves protruding from the base, an array of fibrous spears, easily five feet long, grew in all directions. Adam ran his hand along one of the spears. It was light. But not brittle. There was strength in the fibers—a balance between resilience and give. He broke one of the stems free with a sharp twist and removed a cluster of buds near the tip. The sun had already done most of the drying, leaving it rigid and pale. He examined it like a craftsman checking a fresh tool—turning it in his hand, gauging the weight.

It wasn't perfect, but it would do. Adam held the spear upright and gave it a slow spin. The desert was beautiful, but it was also wild. And wild things had teeth. Adam returned to his camp, where he stowed the spear within reach. At dusk, he lit a fire and prepared dinner. When he had finished, he cleaned his utensils, journaled, and then crawled into his bivy where he drifted off to sleep.

FIFTY-NINE

THE DESERT SHIMMERED in the glow of early morning. Wind skimmed across the dunes, leaving shifting ridges like ripples on a massive, sleeping beast. Adam had been awake for an hour. He left his bivy at first light and stood near the edge of the canyon, watching the Tharnak perform a slow, meditative walk across a flat bed of stone. Six of them moved in wide arcs around a central spire—each step deliberate, their heavy legs sending pulses through the ground like a drumbeat made of earth.

He sat on a shelf of sun-warmed rock, his makeshift spear resting across his lap. Then, the sand moved. At first, it was subtle. Then came the sound: a hiss, like air escaping under pressure. Adam stood. The Tharnak froze mid-step, their fronds flaring outward in warning.

The sand erupted.

A creature burst from beneath the surface—massive, scaled, and seething. Its body coiled like molten steel. It was easily twenty yards long, the color of scorched copper. Fins fluttered at its sides, and its eyeless head reared back, its jaws wide, revealing rows of thin, needle-like teeth. The serpent let out a sound that tore across the desert. The

Tharnak moved instantly. Three charged forward, slamming into the serpent with bone-rattling force. The others circled wide, coordinating their attack.

But the serpent was fast. It coiled and lashed out, flinging one of the Tharnak into the rock wall with a shuddering crack. Another was bitten mid-charge—its armor torn away by a twist of the serpent's jaws.

Adam sprinted into the fray. The injured Tharnak thrashed in the sand, its legs twitching, its bodily fluid running dark against its sandstone-colored plates. The serpent reared for the killing blow.

Adam walked with his spear raised. The serpent turned toward him. Its head struck swiftly—Adam rolled to the side, avoiding the impact. He came up fast and plunged the spear deep into the creature's flesh.

A scream, shrill and wet, burst from the serpent. It twisted violently, the shaft of the spear snapping in Adam's hands as it convulsed. The Tharnak were on the beast in an instant. Three of them struck in unison, driving their massive bodies into the writhing coils of the creature, pinning it to the ground. One of them—small and fast—delivered the final blow, a downward stomp that cracked the serpent's skull with a sickening crunch.

The desert went still. The dust settled. The Tharnak did not move.

Adam staggered back, panting, his eyes wide, his body shaking. He looked down at his hands, covered in blood—some his, most not.

Then he saw it. The fallen Tharnak. The one that had taken the brunt of the first strike. It lay in the sand, still. Its fronds limp, its chest plates cracked open.

The others gathered around the body with their heads bowed. The air grew thick with sorrow. Adam stepped forward to join them. The Tharnak began moving slowly in a wide circle, their feet stomping out a pattern that reverberated through the canyon floor. Adam felt the rhythm. He stepped in line, mimicking their pace, placing his boots where their feet had fallen. His stride was smaller and lighter, but his intention matched theirs.

As he walked, the sorrow they radiated settled in his chest. The body of the fallen Tharnak was lifted by two others and carried to a shallow depression near the canyon wall.

There, without fanfare, it was laid gently into the earth. The others stood around it. A final stomp—in unison—sent a pulse through the ground so strong Adam felt it rattle in his bones. The ceremony ended with silence. And Adam knew their bond had changed.

SIXTY

THE CANYON WAS quiet the next morning. The wind had stilled. The sand no longer whispered. The serpent's body had been dragged away, leaving only a smooth swale in the soil—a scar half-swallowed by shifting sand. Adam had broken camp and stood with his pack shouldered. The air was cool and dry; the sun had not yet risen above the cliffs. The Tharnak gathered near the canyon's edge, silent as ever, their fronds still. One of them approached—larger than the others, with scarred plating along its side. It stepped close and extended its appendage. Adam met it without hesitation. A slow wave passed between them, which Adam understood as a sign of permission. What lay ahead was not forbidden, but it was sacred. When he had arrived in the desert and showed no malice, he was accepted, but now he was trusted.

Then, an image formed in Adam's mind: a shoreline, shimmering in morning light, threaded with veins of pink water. Adam broke the connection, nodded once, and whispered, "Thank you."

The Tharnak did not respond but stood still while he turned toward the south.

The descent to the sea was less steep than the drop-off from the plateau. The harsh desert gave way to sloping ridgelines and then to fields of brittle rock carved by ancient rivers. Adam hiked for hours, losing altitude gradually, passing strange pillars of twisted sedimentary stone and alien plants. He paused and filled a bottle from a cold spring that bubbled from the rocks. He inspected the water with a flashlight. As always, it carried the faintest hue of rose.

By midday, he caught sight of the river cutting across the landscape. Shimmering light reflected off pools that ran out toward the ocean. Adam trekked along a ridgeline eastward. The land sloped gently into a shallow basin—toward a series of tidal shelves where the river spilled into the sea. He calculated there were still a few hours before dusk—enough time to explore the shoals before making camp. The terrain was open here, sun-drenched and humming with life. Not quite sea, not quite swamp. A liminal space between biomes.

Arriving at the water's edge, he removed his boots and socks and stepped barefoot into the shallows, the warmth of the water wrapping around his ankles like silk. The ground beneath his feet, firm in some places, soft in others, rippled with fine silt and was scattered with smooth stones. Luminous strands of algae floated in the current, gently swaying with the tide. They glowed like threads of captured starlight, their tendrils trailing behind them.

Clusters of bell-shaped polyps rose from the riverbed, opening and closing in hypnotic motion. They pulsed with vibration—a musical oscillation that Adam felt in his feet. He crouched beside one and reached out to touch it. It recoiled at first but, a moment later, resumed its rhythm.

Small, translucent, finless fish flashed through the water. One paused near his leg and hovered, its body flickering with bursts of color, then strayed away like a thought that could not be caught.

Further out, a coral-like shelf jutted from the water, coated in what looked like tiny breathing mouths. They opened and closed in overlapping patterns, drawing in water and exhaling it again in cool spirals. When Adam placed a hand upon the surface, it exhaled gently against his palm—like a sigh.

All around him, life bloomed. He had not known what he might find here, but he never expected this. He spent hours there. Walking the shoals. Kneeling in pools. Listening. Touching. Waiting. Each moment deepened the feeling that this place was not just alive—but aware.

He lay back in one of the pools, the water shallow and warm, and let the current surround him. Tiny lifeforms skated over his skin—curious, and unafraid. He closed his eyes and listened to the layered hush of sounds.

He stayed until the sun was near the horizon. The air grew heavier. The harsh crimson light softened to amber, casting the shallows in firelit tones. The algae dimmed. The polyps' rhythm slowed. Adam sat at the edge of a wide basin and watched the light shift across the water.

He was soaked. His clothes clung to him like a second skin, but he didn't care. He felt more himself here than he had anywhere since arriving on Opturius. He didn't feel like a visitor, or an explorer.

He was a participant.

SIXTY-ONE

THE STORM HAD LONG PASSED, but the ship still shuddered now and then—subtle creaks in the hull as if it were remembering what it had survived. Major Harris stood in his bunkroom. Chief Systems Engineer Schmidt, a thin man in his forties with short red hair, stood beside him, holding a diagnostic slate.

"I'm not gonna sugarcoat it, Major" he said. "We have problems. The left undercarriage locking strut didn't fully engage during power-down. I think the surge from the storm blew one of the magnetic dampeners mid-cycle. It's sticking."

"How bad?"

"Bad enough that if we lift off and try to land again—on anything other than a level-grade pad—we could collapse the strut completely. Best case, we stay grounded. Worst case…" He let the sentence trail off.

Harris frowned. "So relocation's out."

Schmidt nodded. "One hard landing and we're not just slightly delayed in returning—we're stranded."

Harris sighed. "I had hoped we could reposition to the desert if Walker can't make it back."

"I had the same thought. Before the storm tried to turn us into a ball of tin foil."

"Then, he's going to have to climb."

Chief Schmidt looked at Harris, his expression softening. "You think he has a chance?"

"If anyone can do it, he can."

SIXTY-TWO

AFTER A NIGHT OF SLEEP, Adam emerged from his bivy, boiled water, and made a cup of instant coffee. Breakfast consisted of a mug of rehydrated hash browns and sausage. He checked the list Harris had given him, hoping he would encounter another form of intelligent life. The next preassigned species name was *Mirenai*. After downing the last of his sad coffee, he returned to the shore.

Mist drifted across the shoals, rising from the warm surface of the water. The world was hushed. Even the creatures of the shallows moved more carefully as if sensing that something was nearby. Adam stepped into the water with care, barefoot again. The sediment gave way under his feet. The warmth of the current welcomed him.

There was a tension of anticipation in the air. He moved slowly, deeper into the water, until it reached his waist. He paused, his eyes scanning the horizon.

There was nothing visible, but he *felt* them. Suddenly, a light beneath the water shifted.

Shapes emerged—slow, elegant motions just beneath the surface. Fluid forms, graceful and complex, weaving in spirals around his legs and torso. Their movement stirred no wake. Their substance glowed softly, translucent and iridescent. Adam stayed still, watching them carefully.

One of them hovered just below the surface, then breached silently, rising into the open air. It had no face and no limbs. Its body undulated, its fluid form folding and unfolding like an underwater blossom. Bioluminescent patterns rippled across its surface. It seemed to look at Adam, though it had no eyes to speak of. He felt as though he was being observed.

Then, Adam felt something pass through him. It left no clear message, only tension and discord. Adam furrowed his brow, trying to parse it. But the more he focused on it, the further it scattered.

More waves followed—irregular, non-repeating, layered like broken music. Low vibrations hummed beneath his ribs. As with the Zenolith and Tharnak, Adam assumed he was being probed until he confirmed his intentions.

"I mean you no harm," he said. He released a slow breath and waited for it.

Then, it came. A warm wave of pressure moved into his abdomen, through his chest, up his throat, and settled just behind his eyes.

The key had been sent. The being drifted closer. Another wave passed through him.

"You came without fear. You trusted the river."

Adam's spirit responded before his voice. "Yes," he whispered aloud, though the words seemed redundant.

"You seek understanding."

"I do."

"Understanding will come. But first—you must listen."

Adam quieted himself. He let his questions go. He let his own story drift into the stillness. He let his spirit lean toward the being—the Mirenai—as if leaning into the wind.

A new pattern had emerged—soft, slow, tremulous. A wave so low it seemed to rise from the seabed and not the creature. Another wave followed—delicate, and unstructured.

Then another.

"You are not here to take. You are not here to conquer."

Adam answered both with a single thought: *Never.*

Then, another wave. "You are welcome here."

More shapes emerged behind the Mirenai, rising like spirits from the deep. Half a dozen others—moving as one. Their forms flowed around him in looping arcs, never quite touching him but always near. Their presence was overwhelming and yet not oppressive—like standing in a cathedral and knowing every column, every arch, has turned to regard you.

The others echoed the same message, forming a circle around him. The water brightened, casting ripples of light across Adam's face.

"I see you brought friends," Adam said.

The Mirenai spiraled in place. Then, Adam heard a clear message. "Come below with us."

He chuckled. "Thank you ... but I can't breathe down there."

Another message: "We mean you no harm."

They had used his own words against him. His mind filled with doubt. Did he doubt his own knowledge, or theirs? He sat there staring at the vermilion water. Then, a thought came to him.

It's not really water. And if it's not water, then what is it?

He remembered the Tharnak "drinking" it. He thought he might have been healed after drinking it. Still, he didn't like the idea of drowning.

The Mirenai hovered before him, waiting patiently. He looked at them, still wrestling with fear.

Quietly, he heard the word, "Trust."

He let out a sigh of defeat.

Harris is gonna kill me, he thought as he slipped into the water with only his face above the surface. His pulse quickened.

"Let go," came the next thought.

Adam floated in the water. He closed his eyes and took a deep breath.

The Mirenai encircled him, then gently wrapped their forms around him and submerged, taking him beneath the surface. Panic gripped him as his instinct to breathe kicked in.

"Breathe," came the next message from the Mirenai.

Adam knew they did not intend to kill him. He felt a familiar pulse in his chest. He tried to relax and took a small breath, allowing the fluid to fill his lungs. It was uncomfortable, but there was no urge to cough. Nor was there an urge to breathe.

Inexplicably, his body was receiving the oxygen it needed from the water. As the realization hit him, he was exhilarated. *I'm breathing underwater? This planet is crazy.*

The Mirenai carried him lower until his body rested on the reef floor. Then, Adam sensed a question. "Why do you bind your river?"

He was confused. *What?*

The next message was a series of visions:

A river. Controlled. Dammed. The flow was choked by the weight of his own intent. Water fought to escape its walls.

The visions struck something inside him. He felt a gentle conviction about his need to tightly manage his affairs and the affairs of those he loved. *I don't mean to control,* he thought.

But even as the thought arose in his mind, the memories followed:

His voice raised with Major Harris.

Objecting to Lisa meeting with a new friend.

A temper tantrum when a coworker ignored his advice.

Insisting things must go his way.

Shame filled him.

The Mirenai responded to his memories. "Control is born of fear. Fear comes from pain."

Adam frowned. *It's not that simple. If I let go, people get hurt. Things fall apart.* A long silence followed. Then, another vision formed in his mind: A current moving freely. Flooding, eroding, and breaking, but carrying life.

Then, he saw a hand clenched tightly around a clump of sand. The tighter it gripped, the more sand escaped.

Another message came, as soft as the tide: "You cannot love what you must control."

His entire life—every plan, every fight, every broken relationship—had been built on the illusion that if he just held on tighter, he could shape the world into something safe. Something predictable. Something permanent.

But people aren't mountains. And love is not conquest. His throat tightened, remembering the choices he had made. Bitterness filled him as he recalled relationships he had destroyed. His body convulsed as each wave of regret and guilt rocked him. *I'm sorry. I'm so sorry,* he thought. The Mirenai held him in that place for some time. He saw in his mind a dam that started to crack. Water began trickling through.

The Mirenai spoke: "You can only control your steps through the water. You cannot control the current, the storm, or the sea. You must learn to trust the unknown."

A thought formed in Adam's mind. *I understand.*

Without warning, the Mirenai began carrying him to the surface. His head emerged, and he swam slowly toward the shallows. Kneeling on the reef, he bent downward and exhaled deeply, letting the pink fluid drain from his lungs. He felt light-headed and slightly nauseous. After a moment, he stood up.

The Mirenai drifted into deeper water, their bodies fading into the mist of the shoals. He watched them go, now feeling peaceful and stronger.

He felt the serenity that comes from accepting that others will make their own choices.

Sometimes, they'll choose poorly.

Sometimes, he'll pay the price for their choices.

But it's not his job to fix them.

The sea stretched before him. And for the first time, he understood that its beauty lies in the fact that it will not be controlled.

SIXTY-THREE

ADAM BROKE camp and left the sea at dawn. He didn't see the Mirenai again—but he had felt their farewell in the harmonic undercurrent of the shallows. They had drifted away as silently as they had come, their light dimming beneath the surface until only their memory remained.

He had lingered a while, standing ankle-deep in the surf, watching the tide sweep pink-tinted foam across the shallows. But the pull was northward now—toward stone and heat of the desert.

He was supposed to be back at the ship by now. Despite that, he didn't take the most direct route back. Instead, he followed a rising path that hugged the inland edge of the coastline. A gentle ridge that curved northward, forming a natural boundary between the sea and the vast, broken expanse of the interior.

At the peak of the ridge, the land unfolded before him.

Adam stood still and absorbed the full breadth of Opturius—the parts he had touched and the regions still unknown. To the south lay the sea, its surface pink and shimmering. To the north, the desert rolled in waves of mauve and rust, fractured by jagged shadows. Further north, the cliffs that led to the plateau rose like a scar in the land—sharp, defiant, uncaring. And beyond them, the mountain range hovered like a memory, still shrouded in perpetual light.

He could see it all.

And it undid him.

He dropped to his knees and wept, his mind reeling from the weight and responsibility of the mission. Every landmark carried a story. Each place held a piece of him now. And still, the path ahead was uncertain. He wiped the tears from his eyes and gazed toward the cliffs. He had barely made it down them alive, but going back up? There was no obvious way, and that was what unsettled him most.

A breeze lifted, dry and quiet, brushing against his face. The scent of the sea clung to his skin, but beneath it was the sharp bite of dust and stone—the breath of the desert that awaited his return.

Adam fell into character. "Well, Wyatt... I reckon our odds are slim to none... but then again, slim's got a habit of flinchin'."

He looked once more across the land, committing it to memory. Then, he slowly stood, turned north, and began his descent toward the desert.

SIXTY-FOUR

THE SHIP'S galley was dim, lit only by the soft blue glow of the wall panels. Private McDermott sat slouched at one of the metal tables, his boots resting on the bench across from him, a half-eaten protein bar in his hand.

Corporal Rodriguez entered, grabbed a tin cup from the rack, and poured herself the closest approximation of coffee the ship could synthesize. She looked at McDermott. "You still brooding about Walker?"

"He's been gone seven days," McDermott said.

Rodriguez blew across the surface of her drink. "I know. But Harris isn't worried."

"Bullshit," McDermott shot back. "You remember how he was when we launched? Full of confidence and totally in control. Now he spends half the day pacing and talking to himself."

"He believes in the guy," Rodriguez said. "For whatever that's worth."

Sergeant Vale stepped into the room, rubbing his eyes. "Adam's alive. His biometric sensor just sent an update." He sat in the vacant seat across from McDermott, set a tablet on the table, and pulled up the latest log. "He must have hit a spot where the signal made it to the ship. Maybe a hill. Vale scrolled. "Look at this. Heart rate steady. Body temp 98 degrees. Oxygen normal."

Lieutenant Harrow leaned forward. "You ever meet someone who was brilliant in one area and a total mess everywhere else?"

"Most of my exes," Vale said dryly.

Harrow chuckled. "Walker's got the instincts. You can't teach that stuff. Either you have it, or you don't. He may be a broken man, but somehow, he just keeps going."

McDermott looked at Harrow. "You know, I keep wondering. Why him? Why not a xenobiologist? A linguist? Somebody who could actually analyze what's happening out there instead of just... some random guy going by his feelings."

"Because nobody's qualified for this," Harrow replied. "You've read Adam's reports. Think about it. What do you do when the mission shifts from 'observe and record' to 'survive contact with the divine'?"

"Sure, he may have instincts, and talent, but there's 4,000 feet of rock between him and us," Vale said quietly.

Harrow looked at Vale. "You think he'll make it back?"

"He should have been killed on the mountain," Vale said, "but he made it back anyway. I don't know, maybe he has nine lives. I *do* know this... I wouldn't bet a round of drinks against him."

"Speaking of drinks," Harrow said, "I think Harris has a secret stash of booze in his quarters. Maybe we can guilt it out of him."

Rodriguez raised her cup. "I'll drink to that. To the ghost in the sand."

Harrow raised his cup. "Hopefully, he leaves his ghosts *in* the sand."

SIXTY-FIVE

ADAM STOOD at the far edge of the desert, where the sea's scent mingled with dust. The terrain had changed, the sand shifting like moods. He stopped near the canyon where he had left the Tharnak. He removed his pack and sat on a flat stone, sipping water. He was running dangerously low on supplies.

He stared up at the cliffs, remembering the route he had taken on the descent. If he could reach the nearest ledge, he could scramble across the boulder field and then up shorter ledges. Each sheer face that he would need to ascend had a rope in place that he had left there. But the nearest ledge was more than a hundred feet from the ground. On the other hand, he had not fully scouted the cliffs from below. Maybe there was a route he had not seen.

He put away his water bottle, shouldered his pack, and moved toward the cliffs, where he set up camp.

Night fell fast.

The stars over the desert were sharp, unobstructed by clouds. He thought he should name some new constellations. A group of stars that aligned to form an elongated oval caught his eye. There were even a couple of stars that formed a tail. "I'm calling you Jester."

Adam crawled into his bivy and closed his eyes, listening to the occasional low vibration echoing through the earth. Tharnak were moving somewhere nearby. He couldn't see them, but he felt them.

And they, no doubt, felt him.

SIXTY-SIX

MAJOR HARRIS SAT ALONE in the comms alcove of the ship, his eyes scanning an array of display screens. A line of static hissed across the secondary band—a frequency reserved for emergency beacons. Then, he heard a sharp tone. He leaned forward, narrowing his eyes.

He tapped a few commands and brought up the waveform. It was only a few seconds long. A burst of data that didn't repeat. No embedded metadata. No clear source. Just a whisper through space. Too ordered for interference.

He frowned and ran it through the signal classifier. Negative match. He adjusted the gain and tried again. Still no ID.

He leaned back, a slow, uneasy breath escaping his chest. The signal had come from the far side of the planet. High angle, diffuse trajectory, possibly refracted.

He toggled the encryption log and recorded the burst with a time stamp and location trace:

    UNCLASSIFIED SIGNAL — ORIGIN UNKNOWN.

Then he scribbled something in his personal notebook:

> *Not native to Opturius. Too structured.*
> *File under: anomalies.*

He closed the log and returned to the primary feed, forcing the puzzle out of his mind.

SIXTY-SEVEN

AT DAWN, Adam was up, exploring the cliffs, looking for a route back to the plateau. He was examining the contours of a rock face, trying to determine whether it could be bolted, when he heard a strange sound. A very unnatural sound. His eyes shot skyward. There, carving a dark crescent across the morning sky, came another ship. It was sleek and angular, not like the ship he now calls home. It was moving fast. Adam stepped into the shade of the cliff and crouched, watching. The vessel descended slowly into the open terrain, landing east of the rock spires, closer to the river. Adam dared not expose himself. He decided to remain hidden until the visitors left.

But what if they don't leave? How long could he remain out of their sight?

He figured the rations still left in his pack would run out in a couple of days. He was anxious to get back to the ship.

Several hours later, the ship's door opened, and four figures emerged. The team's movements were efficient and rehearsed—not the hesitant actions of explorers inspired by awe, but the casual aggression of men who believed nothing could challenge them.

At the front strode Colin Drexel—alpinist, author, public intellectual of the worst kind—a man who'd built a career by using others to place him on untrodden ground, then selling the story as if he alone had conquered the unconquerable. His eyes scanned the desert as if he already owned it.

He turned in a slow circle, then knelt and ran his hand through the sand. "Do you feel that? Conductive. There's something beneath us. Networked. Resonant. I'd wager ten-to-one this planet is wired up like a cathedral."

A crewman walked ahead and paused. "Hey. You see that?"

The others turned.

Across the basin, several substantial forms were approaching slowly, rising from the rocks like phantoms made flesh.

Five Tharnak approached the strangers.

The lead Tharnak stopped at the edge of a low ridge. Its fronds pulsed outward in slow, rhythmic vibrations—an unmistakable signal to anyone with even the slightest intuition.

But intuition was in short supply today.

"You think they're dangerous?" one of the crew asked.

"Sentient, maybe," said another, raising a scanner.

Drexel walked toward the Tharnak without any hesitation. "I don't need a readout to know they're intelligent. Look at the formation. The symmetry. They're communicating."

He stopped twenty feet away and raised a hand in mock greeting.

The Tharnak didn't respond.

Drexel tilted his head. "Hostile?"

Still nothing.

"They're waiting for something," said one of the crew, fidgeting with his belt.

"They're deciding," Drexel replied, half smiling. "Whether we're gods or parasites."

Adam watched Drexel's team until they returned to their ship hours later. He had hoped to find an ascent route today, but that would have to wait. The Source warned him they were coming. And now, they were here. But for how long? He returned to his bivy and crawled inside. Tomorrow, he'd have a decision to make.

SIXTY-EIGHT

THE ZIPPER of the bivy rasped open, its sound sharp against the morning stillness. Adam stepped out into the blush of early light, stretching his arms against the bite of the morning air. A breeze moved across the sand, dry and low, carrying the sound of intruders.

Adam would have preferred not to be seen, but the ship's sensors would have detected him eventually. An encounter with Colin Drexel seemed unavoidable.

I can't stay here forever. I'm almost out of food. Might as well get it over with, Adam thought. He left camp, walking until he had passed the easternmost spire and then made his way toward the ship.

Drexel's team had begun offloading their gear, which was contained in sleek, black crates. The ship, silver and without a blemish, stood beside the river.

Three of the crew members moved briskly, establishing perimeter sensors and laying out their terrain mats. Another worked on calibrating a drone. A fifth figure emerged—broad-shouldered, camera-friendly, wearing a grin.

Drexel spotted Adam and raised a hand. "Well, if it isn't the Ghost of Summits Past."

Adam looked at Drexel, unimpressed. "Didn't expect to see you here."

"Didn't expect to be here. But my skills were needed." He spread his arms. "So—here I am."

Adam rolled his eyes. The mountaineering community is small enough that after a few years, you run into all the biggest names. Drexel was more famous than most due to his ability to attract film crews. Adam, on the other hand, shunned the limelight.

"No offense, Walker, but you look like hell. When was the last time you had a shower?"

"I took a swim a couple days ago."

Drexel scanned the desert and noticed Adam had no equipment or crew with him. "So, you really went feral out here, huh? No team. No drones. That's commitment."

Adam stared at Drexel. "I'm on a tight budget."

Drexel gestured to the desert behind them. "So, what's it like?"

Adam raised an eyebrow. "You landed on it. You tell me."

"You know what I mean," Drexel said, lowering his voice a bit. "You've obviously been here for some time, is there sentient life?"

Adam despised Drexel's smugness, but he understood the forces at play on Opturius. He knew the intruders were in a position of vulnerability, even if they did not. And he felt any information he divulged to Drexel would, in the end, not harm the planet or its inhabitants.

"I've found five intelligent species so far," Adam said at last.

"No kidding? How did you communicate with them?"

Adam looked past him toward the distant cliffs. "You wouldn't believe me if I told you."

Drexel followed his gaze, squinting against the light. "Try me."

Neither man said anything nor moved for a long time. Drexel shifted uncomfortably. "Hey, Walker, you in there? I think the sun may have gotten to you," he said impatiently.

At last, Adam spoke his mind: "This place doesn't appreciate ego. It honors humility."

Drexel smirked. "Good line. You writing poetry now?"

Adam stood there with his arms crossed.

Drexel clapped his hands together. "Well, how about we get you aboard our ship? Swap stories, compare notes. Living out here in the wild, you must be dying for something clean and climate-controlled."

Adam hesitated. He could see the angle already—Drexel would mine his notes and present them to his bosses. Another shortcut. Another amazing feat accomplished by capitalizing on someone else's sacrifice. But he was nearly out of supplies, and he didn't know how he would get up the cliffs. Perhaps this was an opportunity.

Would Drexel help me get back to the plateau?

He still didn't like it, but he relented. "Fine."

Drexel smiled. "Perfect. I'll have coffee ready."

As they walked toward the ship, Adam glanced at the river, its surface still and gentle.

SIXTY-NINE

MAJOR HARRIS SAT on the edge of his bunk, his elbows resting on his knees, his palms pressed together. The lights were dimmed, casting the room in shadow. Outside, the wind howled across the plateau.

Adam should have been back four days ago. Harris told himself there were perfectly reasonable explanations for him not returning yet—terrain, equipment failure, weather—but none of them felt sufficient. He leaned forward and rubbed a hand down his face, the stubble rasping beneath his fingers.

"I shouldn't have sent him." The admission tasted bitter.

He'd read Adam's file a dozen times before the launch. Capable. Intuitive. Resilient. But haunted. Harris thought the opportunity to explore Opturius on his own, without a deadline or clients, might heal his brokenness and lift him back into the saddle. That's what he told himself, anyway. Though he did give Adam a deadline. Perhaps that was the issue. Maybe he was still being defiant.

In truth, he wasn't sure if it had been his keen insight or merely desperation that led him to choose Adam. Now, the silence was making him pay.

He stood and crossed to the far wall, where a narrow storage panel had been left half open. Inside was the pack he'd prepped for search and retrieval. Just in case. It sat like a silent accusation—a backup plan for a choice he couldn't undo. He pulled it halfway out, then stopped. He stared at it. With a sigh of resignation, he turned away from the pack and sat on the bed. "You better not be dead, Walker."

SEVENTY

COLIN DREXEL'S ship interior was antiseptic. Bright, sleek, and orderly. Everything had a sheen—stainless steel surfaces, silent diagnostics screens, and gear stacked in precise modular cases.

Adam sat across from Drexel at a table in the galley, a steaming mug between his hands. Water bottles and protein bars were arranged neatly between them. Drexel, ever the host, leaned back, his boots casually planted on the floor, his hands behind his head. "So, Adam, exactly how long have you been here?"

"I'm not sure... maybe a month."

"All that time out here without a lab, no evac support, no camera crew to document your suffering?"

"You know I prefer to work alone."

Drexel smirked. "Suffering in solitude always was your game." He reached into his pack and pulled out a tablet. "Look, I'll cut to it. You said you found intelligent life. That's big."

Adam stared at him. "I didn't find it. It found me."

"Sure." Drexel grinned. "That's a matter of semantics. What I need to know is how you communicated."

Divulging to Drexel the things he had learned about Opturius violated everything Adam stood for. Reflexively, he resisted the request. But then, an internal tug begged him to reconsider—a voice that suggested Drexel was playing a losing hand. Adam surrendered.

"The species I've encountered communicate, but not with audible sounds. The Zenolith—a species of living mineral columns—communicate through visual imagery. The Tharnak, whom you've already met, communicate through vibration. The Mirenai—an aquatic species—communicate using something like sonar. Then, there's the river and the mountain. The river is alive. It doesn't just communicate, it evaluates. At its source, on the mountain, there's a place. Hard to describe, but there's another species there that communicates through song."

"Fascinating," Drexel replied. "How did you manage to decode it all?"

"I listened."

Drexel blinked. "You... listened?"

Adam nodded. "Not with my ears. It's not audible. You have to tune your soul to their frequency and the mode they're using and listen. Eventually, they will transmit a key that unlocks the meaning of their messages."

"God, you always were the mystical type. All that ascetic garbage. The summit is sacred, blah, blah, blah."

Adam stared at Drexel.

Drexel set down the tablet and folded his hands. "Look, Adam. I do respect what you've done. Really. You paved the way. But the people who pay the bills aren't interested in mysticism. They need analysis. Application. Strategic insight. So, here's the deal—give me your raw notes. I'll filter them into a working model. I'll credit you. Then, everyone wins."

"I'm not trying to win."

Drexel rolled his eyes. "Come on, Walker. We're not kids anymore."

"No, we're not." Adam stood slowly, setting the mug aside.

Drexel straightened. "That's it?"

"Look, you've got what you came for. I told you what I've seen and what I learned. But I feel a warning is in order."

"Oh boy." Drexel leaned back in his chair again. "Let me guess. The planet is angry?"

"Not angry. Discerning might be a better word. It evaluates."

Drexel laughed aloud. "So, the mountain's grading me? You serious? What's it gonna do—fail me?"

"I see a D minus in your future."

Drexel just sat there. Adam had finally silenced him.

"This isn't a joke, Colin. When I got here, I felt a presence. It was always watching me. Always evaluating me. I feel it now. Don't you?"

"The only thing I feel is hungry. I guess I'm just not tuned in," Drexel said sarcastically.

"Opturius understands our motives—when we've come to take, or when we've come to serve."

Drexel scoffed. "You sound like a priest."

"You don't understand what you're dealing with. My advice is to head back to Earth and forget you ever came here."

Drexel's eyes narrowed. "Oh... one more thing, Walker. Where *is* your ship, anyway?"

Adam looked at him calmly. "I took the bus." He picked up two water bottles and three bars from the table and shoved them into his pockets.

He lifted his mug to his lips and took a quick gulp. "Thanks for the coffee." He turned and walked toward the exit.

SEVENTY-ONE

ADAM STEPPED out of the ship and back into the blood-stained world of Opturius. Behind him, the ship's outer door hissed shut. He didn't look back. The soil shifted beneath his boots. The river murmured faintly behind him, slow and unhurried. Five minutes after leaving the ship, he noticed a subtle change in the air. The kind that makes birds go quiet before a thunderstorm. Adam turned his eyes toward the sky. He saw nothing unusual. No clouds. Just the vast, violet expanse overhead.

He continued walking. *Drexel hasn't changed,* he thought. *He's still an arrogant fool.* Adam wasn't angry, and that surprised him. An unfamiliar peace had settled over him. The Mirenai had helped him see that the choices of others were not within his control and not his problem. All he could do was control his responses to the words and actions of others. He heard laughter from the other camp. Loud voices and the click of carbon-fiber crates. The desire to control. They were moving quickly, trying to master a planet that hadn't invited them.

Adam found a place to rest. Reclining against a warm stone, he tilted his head toward the spire a hundred yards south of him. A burst of blue light suddenly blazed from atop the spire. The ground shifted. He felt a deep tremor like the beat of a distant drum. He sat up. The dust around his boots was moving. He turned his eyes toward the far ridge where the plateau dropped off in jagged shelves.

The river below the cliffs was no longer murmuring. It was rising.

A crew member from Drexel's ship called out—his voice clipped by distance. Another answered with urgency. There was movement now—and shouts, the sound of boots pounding the earth, and equipment being dragged hastily toward the ship.

Adam stood up and gazed at the cliffs. The flow of water had suddenly surged as if a massive storm had dumped millions of gallons of rain into the river. The waterfall was choked with silt and debris. Pink liquid surged down the channel carved into the desert, finding its course as if it had only been sleeping.

Drexel's team saw it too late. The ship sat dangerously close to the river. Drexel stood outside the ramp, shouting orders and gesturing. His voice was lost in the sound of shifting earth. A technician sprinted for the hatch.

He didn't make it.

The first wave struck the lower fuselage and lifted the ship four feet off the ground. Then the second came, broader and deeper, sweeping the land like a hand across a table.

Cables snapped, equipment vanished. Men, metal, and mission merged into mayhem.

The ship wasn't crushed. It was erased.

The surge lasted only a few minutes. When it was done, the ship was gone, and so were the voices.

Adam stood watching.

Twenty minutes later, the desert was quiet again. As if nothing had happened at all. Adam walked east and knelt beside the river, just beyond the reach of the flood line. The water had receded, but its mark remained—a jagged crescent of silt, debris, and silence.

There was no wreckage. No bodies. No smoke curling skyward to bear witness. Only the sound of the current, carrying away the last breath of those who refused to listen. He watched the surface ripple, a glint of pink light moved across the shallows. Somewhere downstream, a piece of fabric surfaced, then vanished. The wind stirred. The river, now calm, curved away toward the sea.

Adam rose, wiped dust from his hands, and walked westward. Once at camp, he lit his stove, warmed some water and rehydrated a package of freeze-dried scalloped potatoes that desperately needed more cheese.

SEVENTY-TWO

ADAM PACKED up his gear and turned his attention back to the task of finding a route to the plateau. There were a thousand possibilities, but the most logical one would be a wall that brought him back to the boulder field, which led to the fixed ropes he had left in place during his descent. He could ascend them easily if he could reach them.

He returned to the section of wall he had been exploring when Drexel's ship landed. One seam in particular looked promising. Suddenly, Adam heard the approach of a Tharnak. He waited, and at last, it stood beside him.

The Tharnak motioned with its frond toward the canyon wall. Adam looked at the cliffs, then turned and followed the beast as it moved toward the canyon. The creature led him to a narrow opening in the canyon wall where a small stream flowed toward the sea. Adam pulled out his flashlight. The water was bright pink. He cupped some in his hands. It was viscous, just like the liquid from the Source.

They went further into the canyon until, at last, it terminated. Hidden in shadow was an aperture carved by the stream—no taller than Adam's chest, a fissure in the rock just wide enough to crawl through.

If the stream's source was the mountain, then perhaps the Tharnak had offered him a way to return to the plateau.

The passage was so narrow that he could not fit through with his pack. If he were going to enter, it would be without his equipment. He looked at the Tharnak for confirmation. Perhaps for comfort. It pointed at the opening with its frond and gave a single, soft stomp.

Adam removed his pack and set it on the ground near the entrance. He extracted a protein bar and put it in his pocket, took a good, long swig of water from one of the bottles, then turned and stepped inside the passage. The Tharnak watched him—its fronds extended in a slow wave of farewell.

The walls were slick, faintly illuminated with veins of bioluminescent algae. The tunnel was dark, so Adam strapped a lamp to his forehead and turned it on. He moved slowly, hunched low, water lapping around his boots. At times, he had to crawl through the thick mineral water— muddy and warm.

As he progressed, the walls closed in. The ceiling dropped. He ducked often, sometimes crawling on his belly over stone ledges slick with growths that shimmered as he passed. He wondered if he would be able to get through the narrow constrictions even without his pack.

How would the Tharnak know about this tunnel? They've certainly never been here.

The miles wore on.

The path of the tunnel led upward with irregular sections of stepped ledges. Sometimes, the tunnel spiraled as if by some ancient rhythm— too regular to be coincidence, too natural to be mechanical. He didn't know how many hours had passed.

He rested once in a pocket of open space in the tunnel where the water pooled in a wide basin. The surface reflected the light from his headlamp in trembling rings. He crouched, splashing water across his face. Then he continued.

The incline steepened. His thighs burned. His breath came harder. His boots slipped on angled stone, so he used his hands, sometimes climbing on all fours.

At one point, he paused to lean against the wall and felt a faint vibration, like the planet's heartbeat. It calmed him, propelling him forward. As he climbed, the air grew cooler. And thinner. The pressure had changed. The current had grown stronger, too.

At last, the passage widened. The ceiling arched into a massive dome. The walls parted like curtains around a single point of light. Adam climbed a series of short ledges fighting the downward flow of water and emerged from the mouth of the tunnel, then scrambled the last few yards, finally stepping into the open air. He stood up, straightening his crumpled and aching body.

The planet Madreon, massive and glowing, greeted him from the horizon. Twilight bathed the plateau in crimson.

He was back.

He walked slowly toward the edge of the cliff, relief flooding every cell in his body. The desert stretched far beneath him. The path of the river traced a glittering ribbon through canyons and valleys, eventually bending toward the shallows and the sea.

He sat down and let the wind wash over him. His eyes searched for the Tharnak for several minutes. Not seeing any, he sent a thought impression out over the desert, hoping it would find its mark.

Thank you.

SEVENTY-THREE

ADAM MADE his way north toward the ship, his feet aching, his clothes damp from sweat and river water. The waterfall was far behind him, its roar replaced by the familiar buzz of the plateau's insects. The entrance to the ship beckoned him, imperceptible unless you knew where to look.

As he reached the invisible wall, the hull flickered beneath his touch—solid, warm, familiar. The door opened, and he stepped inside.

Major Harris met him at the entrance with a grateful smile. He shook his head slowly. "Walker, you're a sight for sore eyes."

"Hey, boss. Did you miss me?"

"I spent 49 dollars on that damn radio. You never used it once."

"You said it was for emergencies. I had everything under control."

Harris took a seat at the desk. "You've got one minute to wash up, then you'd better start talking."

"You really are an all-work, no-play kind of guy, aren't you?" Adam called over his shoulder as he walked to the bathroom.

"My wife hated it," Harris said from his chair.

"You're *married*?"

"I was. Long story. I'm sure your marriage will be better. Are you done in there yet?"

Adam returned to the dayroom and took a seat at the desk. He began with the Tharnak, explaining how they speak through vibration, and their strength is in the way they honor those who survive adversity.

He told Harris about the two creatures that fought to the death, the battle with the serpent, the death of the Tharnak, their mourning ceremony, and the fierceness of the desert. He described the Mirenai, who taught him the lesson he'd been running from his entire life. That he could not control others. Only himself.

He described the arrival of the second landing party and how the planet did what it does best: protect itself.

When Adam had finished, Harris said, "So let me get this straight. You bonded with a desert war tribe, slew a serpent, had a religious experience with sea ghosts, and crawled four thousand feet through a tunnel carved by God-knows-what to get back here?"

"Pretty much," Adam said, then adding, "Oh... and I dislocated my shoulder on the final rappel when the bolt pulled out of the wall. That was fun."

Harris sighed and rubbed his eyes. "How much gear did you lose?"

"All of it."

Harris looked at him with incredulity. "Everything?"

"I left the ropes hanging from the cliffs. And I couldn't fit the pack through the escape tunnel. So, I left it in the desert."

"It's all replaceable." Harris said. "You're not." He paused. "You okay?"

Adam nodded slowly. "Yeah. I am."

"Anything else?" Harris asked.

"There's one more thing. The desert has columns made of karethite. Hundreds of them. Some are three or four hundred feet high. A couple were more than a thousand feet high. I climbed one."

"Of course you did."

"I never met a lighthouse I didn't want to climb," Adam said, grinning. "Anyway, after I climbed to the top, I found a large stone covered in dirt. I brushed it off. As soon as I touched the stone, it sent a bolt of light that traveled to the other columns. They all lit up. Then, I went into a trance and saw what I think was the history of the planet. I saw the Zenolith when they were born, the Aerum zipping around between the spires, and then, an attack on the planet. The spires went dark, the Aerum fled to the mountains, and the Zenolith went into hiding."

Harris processed the information, then finally asked, "What do you think the purpose is for the lights on the stone columns?"

"I'm not sure, but get this... just before the river washed away Drexler and his stooges, one of the spires fired off a pulse of light. Seconds later, the flood came."

"So, a communication array?"

"Maybe a planetary defense mechanism." Adam stood and stretched. "I'm dying for a shower. I'll brief you on the rest later." He walked toward the bathroom.

Harris sat at the desk, looking at the drawing Adam had taped to the wall. "Welcome back, Walker."

SEVENTY-FOUR

The rain came without wind or thunder,
no warning cry, just drops of wonder,
landing on stone near the mountain's crown.
The world paused, and time slowed down.

Near the Source—the river's head—
the drops touched down, where pilgrims tread.
The glow from the flow pulsed in reply,
a deep pink surge, a cosmic sigh.

More drops followed, soft and shy,
in gentle rhythm—a lullaby.
Spattering ridges and cliffs on high,
then soaking soil where succulents lie.

From crevice and crust, small creatures crept,
their antennae raised, their silence kept.
The chirr of insects deepened, refined—
as if they shared one song, one mind.

The droplets danced on darkened leaves,
then perched on petals like silken sheaves,
and gathered in hollows of root-bound blooms,
on sunlit plains, in shaded tombs.

A Zenolith stood beneath the sky,
its skin still dark, its surface dry.
Deep within, colors stirred unseen—
first blue, then violet, then into green.

The rain traced paths along its spine
in mirrored arcs and scarlet lines.
Each rivulet sang a sacred tune,
like carols crooned beneath the moon.

In the desert, 'neath ridges bare,
where wind wore down the bones laid there,
rain met the sand, then slipped away—
to awaken life beneath the clay.

Seedpods flexed from ancient sleep,
and microbes stirred in caverns deep.
Dry roots drank the falling grace,
the earth absorbed its wet embrace.

A Tharnak raised its regal head,
turning toward the heavens, red.
Its fronds twitched, it turned to hear—
a whispered song was drawing near.

Life's hush returned, but not the same—
the desert now recalled its name.
The spires sang in wind-worn rhyme,
their tune a thread through space and time.

At last, the rain reached out to sea.
Across the reefs, where fish swim free,
it stirred the tide and fell in sheets,
in rings of pink through coral streets.

The Mirenai rose to meet the sound,
their bodies swaying, safe, unbound.
They danced amid the current's flow—
trusting what they did not know.

No war was fought, no storm was hurled—
just echoed peace across the world.
A gift, not earned, yet freely given—
the planet sighed, its sins forgiven.

From cliff to sea, life found its voice
and knelt beneath the clouds, by choice.
As sky kissed soil, its thirst to quell,
Opturius sang, the pink rain fell.

SEVENTY-FIVE

IN THE SUBTERRANEAN heart of Washington D.C., Doctor Evelyn Clark approached her destination. A black SUV slowed to a stop at the gate, where uniformed guards emerged from the outpost. Badges were scanned. Faces were matched. The gate creaked open.

Dr. Clark stepped out of the vehicle, her stride clipped, her expression anxious. The corridors that had once felt secure now seemed cold—like a veneer of control over something that was unraveling.

She passed through the same sequence of badge scans, retinal checkpoints, and biometric clearances until, at last, the final vault door opened. A single guard held it for her.

Inside, the SCIF was just as Clark had remembered it. Sterile and annoyingly quiet.

Agency Director Matthew Lohmeyer sat waiting. His gaze lifted when Clark entered, and she could tell—by the set of his jaw, the way he straightened in his seat—that he suspected this wasn't good news.

She took the chair across from him.

He didn't waste time. "Doctor Clark."

"Director."

"You have an update on the program?"

Evelyn folded her hands on the table. "I do. As you're aware, space travel is a risky proposition. Sending a team to an unexplored planet is riskiest of all. Shortly after the team landed on Opturius, we lost contact with them."

Lohmeyer's eyes narrowed. "Permanently?"

"We're not sure. Automated telemetry signals had been received for roughly 24 hours after landing, then the signals ceased."

"What's the status of the ship?"

"It's unconfirmed, but our engineers believe it was destroyed."

Lohmeyer sighed, his fingers steepled beneath his chin. "Do we know what caused it?"

"No, sir."

Then, Director Lohmeyer asked, "In your estimation is this... tragedy recoverable?"

Evelyn hesitated. "Perhaps," she said at last. "But we'll need to adjust the mission's expectations."

"We can't afford another failure," Lohmeyer said.

"No," Evelyn replied. "We can't."

Lohmeyer nodded once, signaling the meeting was over. He didn't thank her.

Doctor Clark rose, turned, and walked out—back through the maze of checkpoints. Her pace remained brisk, but the quiet behind her felt like a curtain drawing shut. She suspected it wasn't equipment failure or unexpected geologic activity that ended Drexel's mission. The planet had tested her team. And they had failed the test.

SEVENTY-SIX

THE SHIP HAD GROWN QUIET. The dayroom was empty. Even the chatter in the lounge—once steady with theories and worries and laughter that was too loud—had gone still.

Adam stood beside his cryo-pod, his arms folded loosely. The clear lid hung open like a question. The lighting in the chamber was dimmed now, soft blue hues illuminating a row of cylindrical sleep units, each wired to the wall like hibernating cells. Harris entered quietly, carrying a tablet in one hand and a silver thermal mug in the other. He didn't speak at first—just walked the line of pods, checking readouts.

"You ready?" he asked Adam.

Adam looked at the pod again. "Honestly, I could use a nap."

Harris smirked and stopped in front of Adam's unit. They stood together in the quiet.

"So, what will happen to Opturius?" Adam asked.

"That remains to be seen. The planet seems to be capable of taking care of itself—a point I will make crystal clear to the brass back home.

They're not bad people. If they were, I wouldn't be here. I suspect they'll do what's in the best interest of all parties."

"You trust them?"

"I don't trust people easily, but they've given me no reason—so far—not to trust them."

Adam looked into his cryo-pod, then back at Harris. "I have one more question, if you don't mind."

"Shoot."

"Did we accomplish what we came here to do?"

"That's a loaded question," Harris said. "Much of the mission's goals are classified, but I can say, you exceeded every goal we had hoped to accomplish." Then Harris chuckled to himself. "By all accounts, you should be dead, Walker. It's a miracle you're here."

Adam got into character. "Well, Major, to be perfectly honest, I never did like the odds against me. It was a fool's errand from the very beginning. But if I may say so, I bluff better than the devil."

Harris blinked and shook his head. "I sure do know how to pick 'em."

Adam and Harris climbed into their pods. The lids hissed as they sealed. Coolant began circulating. And as the lights dimmed further, the ship prepared to sleep—with two men aboard whose fates had become intertwined in more ways than they presently understood.

EPILOGUE

THE COFFEE SHOP was located across the street from a park that bordered the bay. A bell above the door chimed as a woman left with a paperback in one hand and a paper cup in the other. The place smelled like espresso and pine. It was raining.

Adam relaxed in a corner booth, facing the window, a plain black ball cap pulled low, warming his hands with a mug of coffee. He watched the street.

A soft chime sounded on his device. The screen flickered to life.

Incoming Message.

He tapped the button. A simple line of text appeared:

"Still walking?" –H.

Adam smiled. He typed back:

"Always."

There was a pause. Then, another incoming message:

> "I need your help with a project. I'll give you the details in person."

The noise of the city buzzed outside. Planet Earth, for all its beauty and brutality, still spun forward under gray clouds and neon lights.

Adam stood, dropped a few dollars on the table, and pulled his coat on. As he stepped into the rain, the crowd didn't notice him.

Somewhere in the city, a message was waiting.

And somewhere in the shadows, the next mission had begun.

ABOUT THE AUTHOR

Dave Hayes, formerly a paramedic of 35 years, taught advanced cardiac and basic trauma life support, high-angle rescue, and community preparedness. Hayes has been writing since 2009 and authoring fiction and non-fiction books since 2013. Dave is known as a public speaker, author, podcaster, teacher, and has written more than twenty books on faith and the spiritual life under the pen name Praying Medic. He lives with his wife, an artist and graphic designer in sunny Arizona.

ALSO BY DAVE HAYES / PRAYING MEDIC

Q Chronicles Series | Dave Hayes
Chronicles Book 1: Calm Before The Storm
Chronicles Book 2: The Great Awakening
Chronicles Book 3: This Is Not a Game
Chronicles Book 4: Only at the Precipice

Meshtastic Made Simple
Emergency Preparedness and Off-Grid Communication

The Kingdom of God Made Simple Series | Praying Medic
Divine Healing Made Simple
Seeing in the Spirit Made Simple
Hearing God's Voice Made Simple
Traveling in the Spirit Made Simple
Dream Interpretation Made Simple
Power and Authority Made Simple
Emotional Healing Made Simple

The Courts of Heaven Series | Praying Medic
Defeating Your Adversary in the Court of Heaven
Operating in the Court of Angels

My Craziest Adventures with God Series | Praying Medic
My Craziest Adventures with God - Vol. 1
My Craziest Adventures with God - Vol. 2

The Gates of Shiloh Series | Praying Medic
The Gates of Shiloh

Charity's Garden

And more...by Praying Medic

Emotional Healing in 3 Easy Steps

God Speaks: Perspectives on Hearing God's Voice

A Kingdom View of Economic Collapse (eBook only)

www.ingramcontent.com/pod-product-compliance
Lightning Source LLC
LaVergne TN
LVHW011929070526
838202LV00054B/4548